The Cheyenne Encounter

Center Point
Large Print

**This Large Print Book carries the
Seal of Approval of N.A.V.H.**

The Cheyenne Encounter

D. B. Newton

CENTER POINT PUBLISHING
THORNDIKE, MAINE

This Center Point Large Print edition
is published in the year 2004 by arrangement with
Golden West Literary Agency.

The text of this Large Print edition is unabridged. In other
aspects, this book may vary from the original edition. Printed in
Thailand. Set in 16-point Times New Roman type.

ISBN 1-58547-476-2

Library of Congress Cataloging-in-Publication Data

Newton, D. B. (Dwight Bennett), 1916-
    The Cheyenne encounter / D. B. Newton.--Center Point large print ed.
        p. cm.
    Originally published: The Cheyenne encounter / Dwight Bennett. 1st ed.
Garden City, N.Y. : Doubleday, 1976.
    ISBN 1-58547-476-2 (lib. bdg. : alk. paper)
        1. Large type books. I. Title.

PS3527.E9178C48 2004
813'.52--dc22

                                                                    2004003638

I

Whenever he rode into this town—which was every other week or so, to report the condition of John Isely's scattered cattle holdings—Will Bonner was sure the place had grown since last time. There was always something he hadn't noticed before: new business houses, new saloons and gambling halls springing up out of the ground like mushrooms, old buildings being added to. Everywhere in Cheyenne, this summer of 1874, there was the busy sound of saw and hammer, and the smell of fresh paint.

And of money . . .

No question about it, a lot of money was either being made or expected, chiefly from the current boom in cattle. The Cheyenne *Daily Leader* never failed to point out, in every issue, the increased numbers of beef being grazed on the rolling hills and in coulees along the Platte and the Laramie and their tributaries. Just wait, the paper said, till the market picked up from the slump that began a year ago, and that was beginning to be called the Panic of '73.

Will Bonner didn't know much about the behavior of the market, but he couldn't see much sign of panic as he rode his sorrel up Carey Avenue and looked at the big new homes there, bought with wealth from Wyoming beef—great wooden structures of two and three stories, with wide verandas and deep lawns and iron fences.

Carey Avenue always made him uncomfortable. Sixteenth Street was his part of town—down along the railroad, with his own kind and the easy atmosphere of dollar-a-room hotels, of swinging doors and beer shields and the hangouts where a working cowhand felt at ease. A tall, well-articulated, and lean-hipped fellow, he had skin burned as dark as his saddle, and straight black hair and eyes that maybe hinted at Indian ancestry somewhere; he felt self-conscious in range clothes and worn denim jacket that belonged more properly in one of the creekbank dugouts that served for range camps, out on Horse Creek or the Chugwater.

Now he stepped down before John Isely's front gate and tied Charlie, his sorrel, to the ring in the iron hitching post. He straightened his jacket, beat the dust from his hat against a knee and put it back on again. The iron gate creaked faintly under his hand and he walked up the flagstones, toward the house with its mansard roof and diamond-shaped window panes, its complex frozen rhythms of scroll-saw decoration dripping from the line of the porch roof. As he was about to set a boot on the broad bottom step, a man he hadn't noticed before heaved himself erect from one of Isely's wicker chairs, came out to the edge of the veranda, and planted himself there, definitely blocking the way.

"What do *you* want?" he demanded harshly.

Even with the advantage of elevation, he wasn't particularly impressive—a little below average height, and loosely strung together. The only thing about him that held attention was the gun, with well-polished wooden grips, that filled the cutaway holster strapped against his left leg.

Will Bonner had seen such men before, men who seemed merely adjuncts to their hardware. But it was not pleasant to see one on John Isely's veranda.

His own gun and holster belt were in a pocket of his saddlebags, where he usually left them when he came calling on John Isely. Now he lowered the boot he had raised, set it on the ground again. "What do I want?" he echoed. "From you, not a damn thing."

It wasn't the answer the other man had expected. His eyes pinched up and he said, "You better come up with something better than that!"

"My business is with Isely," Bonner said coldly. "And you sure as hell ain't him!"

"No, but I'm the one you're talking to!"

In as few words as that, it appeared they had got themselves into a confrontation. Bonner hesitated, a little astonished at the posture things had taken and wondering how in the world to defuse it without seeming to back down from the bantam rooster on the porch.

Then someone was approaching across the clipped green lawn, from the direction of a graveled drive that ran beside the house. They both turned as this man spoke sharply. "Spence, what seems to be the trouble?"

Spence answered with belligerence. "I don't know this smart-talking sonofabitch, and he seems to think he's going to walk by me without explaining himself."

"I know him. He works for the boss's new partner. The name is Bonner; he's Isely's foreman."

"Oh." That seemed to take some of the wind out of him. But the gunman was still scowling. Will Bonner, who had now seen a buggy waiting in the drive, turned to face the new arrival. "I take it Rome Patman's in the house, then," he remarked, without warmth. "I've noticed before—anywhere he is, Cowley, you're generally around."

"I do my job," the other answered.

Blond, ruddy-cheeked, clean-shaven, Morgan Cowley always seemed to move with a smooth confidence, tempered by a certain caution in the watchful cast of pale blue eyes. The few times they had met, Will Bonner had developed a keen distrust of this man, whose job could only be described as gunhand and personal bodyguard to his employer, Rome Patman; but Bonner knew enough to respect him as well. Now, the thrust of a thumb indicating the one who stood above them on the porch, he demanded bluntly, "And what about *him?* Are you hunting in pairs now?"

"Vic Spence does his job, too," Cowley told him.

"I'd say he works too hard at it! If you don't want to see him in trouble, better call him off!"

That got a black stare from the smaller man, but Cowley only shrugged. "It's all right, Spence. He's legitimate—he has business with Isely. You can let him by."

"Thanks," Bonner said curtly, and started up the half-dozen broad steps.

For just a moment he thought Spence would refuse to move aside. Obviously it roweled him; but he had received a direct order and he had no choice. Still scowling, the little man drew back and Will Bonner walked past him, without another look. As he reached the door he heard Morgan Cowley say, to his back, "They're in what they call the drawing room." Not bothering to answer, he opened the screen and stepped inside.

He had been working for John Isely far too long to allow of any formality—"When you want me," his boss always said, "just walk in. If you don't see me, try my study at the end of the hall." Nevertheless he felt a trifle in awe, even now, of the dark, high-ceilinged hallway with its carpet and pictures on the walls, the banistered stairway to upper regions. He eased the screen silently shut against a heel, as he pulled off his hat and stood listening a moment.

It was considerably cooler here than in the sunblasted street. As Cowley had predicted, he could hear a rumble of voices beyond the open door of the drawing room. Bonner moved forward and had to duck his head to step through the tasseled archway, where he paused.

John Isely was talking, gesturing with the stem of an unlighted briar pipe. He caught sight of Bonner and said at once, in his booming voice, "Come in, Will—come in. You're the man we need to talk to. Vin was just serving tea," he went on, an expansive gesture beckoning his foreman into the room. "Let her pour you a cup."

"Thanks just the same," Bonner said quickly, but too late. Lavinia Isely, seated at the center table with her silver tea things before her, was already filling another cup. Mumbling a refusal of sugar or cream, he stepped reluctantly to accept it from her.

It was not merely that the eggshell thinness of cup

and saucer made him conscious of his own clumsy and rope-toughened hands; something about John Isely's young wife, with the cornflower-blue eyes and hair like spun gold, seemed to him as fragile as her chinaware. Yet the fingers that he touched briefly were cool and competent, and so was the polite smile she gave him.

He had never seen her that she wasn't wearing that impersonal smile, unperturbed and seemingly untouched by anything that went on around her. His boss had brought a beauty back from Cincinnati with him, sure enough; but Will Bonner had a feeling, after six months, that he would never really know what lay behind that placid brow and smooth, curved cheek.

"Have a seat, Will," Isely said.

Bonner shook his head at the thought of placing his dusty clothing in one of those new wing chairs. "Thanks," he said. "But I been riding, and it feels good to stand. I was at the Clear Creek camp this morning when Red Jackson found me, with the message you wanted me to come in."

"Any trouble at Clear Creek?"

"No trouble. Everything's smooth there."

"Who we got working that camp?" the older man wanted to know.

Bonner named three of their men—all the crew necessary, on that open Wyoming range, to do the necessary chores for a thousand head of beef strung out and feeding on the grass along a tributary creek bottom. "By the way," he added, "after I'd talked to Red I told him to ride on over to Owl Butte. We needed a man there—Dan Hartley got himself throwed, and bunged up a leg."

"The doctor seen Hartley?"

"It's nothing that serious. He'll be in the saddle again, inside a week; but right now it's left Owl Butte short-handed. So, I sent Red."

Despite the questions, it seemed to Will Bonner that Isely was asking them out of habit and, in fact, giving his answers only perfunctory attention. A spare, deep-chested man, with shrewd brown eyes above neatly trimmed whiskers that were shot with gray, he stood now tapping his teeth with the bit of his cold pipe and staring at the carpet; and his mind seemed elsewhere. This was not like other briefings, when he had taken real and keen interest in everything his foreman could tell him about the dozen far-flung cow camps where his thousands of head of cattle ranged, all the way from the South Platte down in Colorado to the Laramie Plain.

Will Bonner didn't like to admit it, but these months since his marriage had clearly changed John Isely.

Now, with his blunt way of getting directly to a point, his boss told him, "Reason I called you in today, I wanted to find out if you'd decided yet where we can best put an additional four thousand new head."

"I figured that might be it," Bonner said. "I told you before, it's a pretty fair-sized herd to throw, all at once, on a range that's filling up like this one around Cheyenne. My best suggestion would still be to break it up into smaller bunches, easier to handle."

"I'm afraid that just won't do," John Isely began, with

a frown; he was seconded at once by the man who, up to now, had sat unspeaking and almost hidden by the wide wings of one of the heavy overstuffed chairs that flanked the fireplace.

"It won't do by any manner of means," Rome Patman declared, with stern emphasis. "That herd is my personal property and I want it intact."

Bonner looked from his employer to the latter's new business partner. "Let me get this straight. I gather what we're talking about is the herd being brought up from New Mexico?"

Isely nodded. "And it's important that it should be kept separate from our own holdings, until the partnership has been formally drawn up and the legal papers signed."

"I see. . . ." He frowned over the matter. "I guess I have to say, then, that Gray's Fork is the likeliest place for them. For one thing, being over the line in Colorado Territory makes it handy for beef arriving from the south. The grass looked good, last time I swung down that way, and there's no other outfits trying to crowd in on us there at the moment. It should do for an emergency."

John Isely appeared to accept the thing as settled. "Good," he said abruptly. "Gray's Fork it is. You'll take care of the details."

"Any idea when I might begin looking for this herd? What brand will it be under? How do I spot it?"

"We got word last night—it's why I sent a rider to fetch you." Isely looked at his partner. "You're the one can best fill him in."

"All right." And Rome Patman got deliberately to his feet.

He shaped up as almost the same height as Will Bonner, but some pounds heavier—the extra flesh of one who led a less active life, and who believed in treating himself well. Still, Bonner had not sized him up as soft in any way. Patman held himself with a strict discipline, as straight as though a ramrod might serve him for a spine. He looked to be in his late forties. His face was chiseled and his mouth, beneath a thick black mustache, was wide without humor.

Eyes with a strange tawny cast to them bore directly on Bonner's as Patman informed him, "The cattle reached the South Platte yesterday evening and are being held there, waiting orders. As you've been told, it's a mixed herd and a large one—four thousand head carrying my road brand, a Slash 6. You'll report to the trail boss. His name is Trace Showalt." Something he saw in Will Bonner's face prompted him to add, "Maybe you've heard of him?"

"I've heard of him."

"That's not surprising," the other said, as though pleased. "Trace Showalt came to me with a reputation as one of the best trail drivers and range foremen in the business—and I can tell you, in the months he's worked for me he's more than lived up to it."

"I reckon," Bonner told him bluntly, "you don't get his kind of reputation without earning it."

He was aware of John Isely's wary frown as he looked back and forth between the two of them, nor did he miss the sudden narrowing of Patman's stare. "Per-

13

haps," the latter said, "you've heard talk that Showalt is tough on the men who serve under him. Well, what *I'm* interested in is results—the kind it takes to run a ranching operation, or hold a herd together on the trail and deliver it intact." He stabbed a forefinger at Bonner for emphasis. "I'll give you odds right now, you'll find that herd tallying not one head short of the number it started with!"

"That's a bet I'd probably lose money on," Bonner said curtly. And not wanting to let this build any further he turned away, with the cup and saucer he was still holding. As he placed them on the table he found himself looking at Lavinia Isely again, to meet that unchanging smile and the calm regard of those serene, too intelligent blue eyes. She indicated the silver teapot but he quickly shook his head. "Thank you, ma'am. No more for me. If I'm gonna make the South Platte tonight, I better be riding."

He looked around, saw his hat where he had placed it on the seat of a lyre-backed chair. As he picked it up, John Isely said suddenly, "But first, Will, there's one other matter of business. Won't take a minute—how about stepping back to the office with me? You'll excuse us," he told his wife and Rome Patman.

Somehow this struck Bonner as clearly a spur-of-the-moment thing. Faintly puzzled, he nodded and let Isely usher him out of the room. Long acquainted with the layout of the big house, he turned left and preceded his boss down the dark hallway to the familiar door.

"Sit down—sit down!" Isely ordered gruffly. "You

can't hurt *these* chairs, at least."

Will Bonner looked at him, saw the grin that told him his employer had understood his problem in the other room. Here, at least, someone of his stripe could feel at home, amid spur-scarred chairs and an old roll-top desk that held a purposeful clutter of papers and ledgers— the heart of Isely's enterprises. Bonner dropped into a leather-seated chair and put his hat on the floor beside him, while John Isely proceeded to fill the bowl of his briar pipe from a humidor containing rough-cut tobacco, tamp it down with one broad thumb, and strike a match.

Watching the pleasure with which he took the first deep drag of smoke and let it out again, Bonner knew this was a sacrifice at the altar of Isley's marriage: Lavinia Isely disliked the stink of tobacco, and his study was now the one room in the house where her husband still felt free to indulge himself in old and smelly habits.

From one wall the mounted head of a six-point buck deer looked down with glassy eyes; on another hung a map of the country around Cheyenne, the colored areas indicating the many strategically located holdings of deeded land controlling hay meadows and line camps and water, which in turn gave Isely command over a good many thousand acres of unfenced open range, scattered over an area almost a hundred miles square. Time, and a lot of canny study, had gone into building that cattle empire.

Tossing the burned match aside, Isely hitched himself onto the edge of the desk and looked at his foreman through a blue-gray burst of smoke. Without warning he demanded, "What were you up to, just now—baiting Rome Patman?"

Will Bonner met his look. "Is that what it looked like?"

"I gotta say, the way you talked about his trail boss . . . and the way he seemed to take it . . ."

The younger man drew a long breath. "Well, you're right, I guess; and if it makes you sore I suppose you got cause to be. Even if I knew Rome Patman well enough to have an opinion about him, it would be none of my business who you take for a partner."

Gesturing, Isely drew a blue line with the smoke trailing from the bit of his pipe. "It's this man Showalt who has you bothered. So, fill me in. What about him? You admit, yourself, he has a good record."

"*Too* good! It just ain't possible for any trail driver to deliver a herd over any distance without taking some losses, but Showalt manages, and there's no mystery how he does it. One of our own men—Bud Dorn— went up the Chisholm with him to Ellsworth, Kansas, for another outfit a couple years back. He's told me that Showalt kept his herd at strength by adding to it all the way up the Trail—and he wasn't too particular how, or at whose expense. He had some tough hands with him, and their only job was to make sure nobody he took from complained too much.

"Bud finally got a bellyful, and when he raised a row over what he'd seen, Showalt had him beaten up and kicked off the drive. He was told he'd be killed if he opened his mouth about anything that had happened.

16

And he didn't he'd learned his lesson."

"He told *you,* though," Isely pointed out, frowning and dubious. "Those are serious charges to be tossed around, Will. You sure he wasn't just talking out a grudge?"

"Bud Dorn's a good man," Will Bonner replied with conviction. "For my money, a dead honest one. I believe him, all right—and when Trace Showalt brings in this herd up from New Mexico, I'm just not gonna be surprised to find some Colorado strays scattered in with it—all wearing Rome Patman's road brand. Don't be surprised, either, if some of his trail crew turn out to be hard-looking customers who obviously never threw a rope at a cow in their lives.

"Even so," he added quickly, "I realize it won't necessarily reflect on Rome Patman. A man can't always be held for what his hirelings do." Which was true enough, of course; though there were questions he could have asked but didn't, about the need Patman seemed to feel for having an armed bodyguard always at hand.

John Isely laid aside his pipe, leaned to open a drawer and bring out a bottle and a couple of glasses. He poured whiskey for them both, handed Bonner his and then sank into his swivel chair, which creaked noisily under him. He eyed his foreman thoughtfully over the rim of the glass as he drained off part of his drink, then set it aside with an impatient gesture. It was clear he had more he wanted to say.

"Will," he began suddenly. "How long you been with me? Six years, ain't it?"

The younger man nodded. "About that."

"And lucky for me! What I knew about cattle, when we started, was too pathetic to mention. When I came out here from Illinois I thought I was going to get into mining—goes to show how things work out.

"We've done real good, too," he added, and swung his chair around so he could look at the big map on the wall. "Not a bigger operation in the Territory, and we started from scratch—a little capital from me, a lot of cow sense from you."

"Don't give me all the credit. It didn't take you long to learn."

"I suppose. . . ."

Isely picked up his drink, finished it off, and sat a moment frowning into the empty glass. Will Bonner waited, knowing his employer was coming to some point and having difficulty with it.

The glass went back on the desk. Isely picked up his pipe again. He turned it in his hands, and then his glance sought the other's face. "Will, you haven't told me so, but I know the idea of me taking a partner has been bothering you. Likely you can't see the sense of it."

Bonner shrugged, uncomfortable and trying to pass it off. "It's your affair."

The older man shook his head. "All the same, you've earned an explanation, and you should have had it before. Well, the honest truth is, I need money—hard cash, and plenty of it. Everything I own is tied up in beef, and after last year's panic there ain't a chance of converting it without taking a bad loss—not until something happens to the market."

He hesitated, rubbing his beard with the bit of the pipe; he seemed embarrassed to continue. "I'll have to admit, too," John Isely blurted, "that I've put quite a lot more'n I expected into fixing this house the way Vin wanted it—but, what the hell! When a man my age is lucky enough to get a woman like her to agree to marry him, it ain't the time to pinch nickels. So, all in all, I'm a little short right now.

"Hell! Why not admit it?" he grunted. "I'm strapped!" He nodded, and puffed a furious cloud from the pipe. "And the banks here are charging three per cent a month—I'm sure as hell not gonna get into *their* hands! That leaves Rome Patman. He has funds to invest in the cattle business, as well as a herd of his own to throw into the pool as soon as Homer Nicholls finishes getting the partnership papers drawn up. Frankly, that money of Patman's is the only quick answer in sight."

Will Bonner frowned. "Isn't a partnership kind of a high price, though? You've been in tight corners before this, John. I've never yet seen one you couldn't find your way out of."

"Maybe." But Isely said it roughly and his manner told Bonner there was more to come. His boss picked up the whiskey bottle and, when Bonner shook his head, started to refill his own glass; then apparently changed his mind, and instead corked the bottle and put it back in its drawer. Will Bonner had a hunch that he was stalling, over something he didn't know how to say.

19

"Will, I don't suppose you'll understand; but I'll try to explain. Lately, something seems to have happened to me. The truth is, being in any business is worth it only so long as a man can see it as a kind of game. And—I dunno. Maybe I been in this one too long. I've kind of lost my taste for it.

"And, there's Vin. She don't really like to have me dealing in cattle, for one reason or another. And she don't like this town. I suppose, with her background, Cheyenne looks pretty raw to her. She'd like us to move to Denver, maybe have me get into some other line of work. . . ."

So now it was out, Will Bonner thought—the thing that was really motivating John Isely's behavior. Behind her polite and smiling façade, Lavinia was watching her chances and having her way. No, Cheyenne would not be good enough for her; this big house on Carey Avenue, with all the money her husband had spent to furnish and decorate it to suit her, would not be good enough because, even here, men like Isely's dusty, horse-smelling foreman could tramp into the house and claim him as one of their own. And John Isely—an older man, enamored of a young and beautiful wife—was bound to see things through her eyes, and bow to her wishes without, probably, even realizing it.

Will Bonner felt a twinge of resentment toward the woman, but he passed that off with a brief movement of his shoulders. No one could help what he was—neither John, nor Lavinia, nor Bonner himself. If the woman gave his old friend a good marriage, and filled a void in his life, that was all anyone had a right to ask for, even if it disrupted familiar and long-standing arrangements.

Still, these had been a good half-dozen years; it was with a sense of something ending that could never be the same that Will Bonner finished his drink. He got to his feet, picked up his hat, and placed his empty glass on the desk. Looking down at his friend, he said, "I guess you know, John, that as far as I'm concerned you can't do anything much wrong. I've enjoyed working for you. Whatever happens now, you'll always carry my best regards."

"Will, I appreciate that!" As though reassured, with a tough scene behind him, John Isely was more like himself again as he swung to his feet. But he was minded of the matter they'd discussed earlier, for he looked narrowly at his foreman as he added, "Then you'll meet that herd? And you'll go easy on any personal feelings you might have about Trace Showalt—or the man he happens to be working for?"

"You got my word on it."

"Fine—fine!" Isely gestured to the door. "This has been a good talk. You go ahead—I'll be right with you." As Bonner opened the door, John Isely was knocking the coals from his pipe before re-entering the part of the house where it was forbidden him now to smoke it.

II

Passing the living-room archway, Bonner glanced in and saw Rome Patman leaning an elbow on the fireplace mantel and chatting pleasantly with Lavinia Isely—Bonner had to admit he looked more at home in such surroundings than he himself, or John Isely for that matter, ever would.

He went on down the hall toward the blast of sunlight beyond the screen door, but before he reached it he heard his name and paused, turning. Patman had followed him, and the man's voice held an irritable edge. "You must be in a hell of a hurry, Bonner!"

"It's a long ride if I want to meet that herd on the South Platte."

"Could be longer if you don't know where to look."

Bonner shrugged. "I figure to find it all right."

"But it's better to be sure."

Alone in the shadowy hallway, these two men faced one another and there was a wary sense of confrontation, of carefully measuring and sizing each other up. It was interrupted as John Isely joined them, stuffing the emptied pipe away into a pocket of his waistcoat. Isely looked at their faces. "Anything the matter?"

"Oh no," his future partner assured him. "I just wanted to suggest that my rider return with Bonner and direct him to where he left the herd. At the same time, he can verify to Trace Showalt that Bonner has authority to act for us."

That made sense to Isely, and Will Bonner had to accept his boss's decision. "All right," he said with a shrug. "Just so it doesn't lose me time. Where do I find this rider?"

"No problem," Rome Patman assured him, and turned to open the screen. "I believe he's right outside."

Morgan Cowley, the ever-present bodyguard, stood leaning against the rail; but it was the little gunman, Spence, who quickly got up from a cane-seated rocker as Patman beckoned.

"This is your man?" Bonner demanded. "He came up with Showalt from New Mexico?" And he turned and looked squarely at Isely, and saw the latter's troubled frown. John Isely would be remembering his prophecy about the crew of the New Mexico herd: by no stretch of the imagination could this tough little man, with the gun nestling against his hip, be taken as an ordinary cowpuncher who belonged with an honest trail outfit.

Bonner didn't make an issue of it, but his distaste was clear in his voice as he asked Spence, roughly, "Where's your bronc?"

"At the livery."

"Get it. I'll pick you up there in half an hour—and I don't want to have to wait." With no more than that he turned away, dragging his hat on straight black hair as he swung away down the steps and the flagstoned path.

As those on the veranda watched the foreman mount and ride out of sight down Carey Avenue, Rome Patman let a frown shape his stern mouth. "What about Bonner?" he said to John Isely. "Is the man part Indian?"

"I wouldn't know. I never asked him."

"He's dark enough to be—and his manner's plenty surly! You claim he's done a good job for you, but I can't say I like him. What's more, it seems clear to me he doesn't think much of this partnership.

"Well, he shouldn't be hard to replace," Patman continued. "I want you to meet this Trace Showalt. He's tough, but he gets results—and he knows how to show respect to his superiors. It could be a good idea to consider him for Bonner's job."

When John Isely had no comment, his new partner let the matter drop.

On entering a Sixteenth Street saloon that tended to be favored by Isely's crew when they weren't on duty, Bonner figured it lucky that he found Pete Gage among the three who were killing time over a bottle and a desultory game of cards. Gage was one of the older hands, steady and sober, and as reliable as any on Isely's payroll. At sight of Bonner he grinned, kicked out a chair for him. "Never seen you relax by daylight before," he declared. "Have a seat. Joe, pour the man a drink."

But Will Bonner turned down both offers. "No time." Standing beside the table, he told his men what was on his mind.

"Four thousand more head!" Gage groaned when he'd finished. "On top of what's already there? Boss, that range on Gray's Fork won't hold 'em!"

"I know. But there's no other place to put them; and orders are they're to be kept together. Looks like we'll just have to move out our own stock and distribute it among some of the other camps. And I'm going to need you boys to help."

The three exchanged a look and Pete Gage said resignedly, "O.K., boss—we'll ride down and make a start gathering cattle. We'll see you there tomorrow?"

"Sometime in the afternoon, I imagine."

Gage scratched a thumbnail through the rasp of whiskers on his gaunt jaw. "Just one question. What about Bud Dorn? With him at the Gray's Fork camp, and knowing what happened once between him and that Showalt—ain't there apt to be some trouble?"

"We'll hope not."

"Maybe, if I could take him an order from you—sending him off somewhere, and out of the way . . ."

The foreman frowned. "I've thought about that," Bonner admitted. "But I'm afraid it wouldn't work. Bud's a proud man; he'd know what I was doing, and he'd resent it—especially if he got the idea I was trying to protect him. No, Bud's got a head on his shoulders. I think we can trust him not to start anything with Showalt."

"Can we say the same about Showalt?" the other insisted. "From all I've ever heard about that sonofabitch, I hate like the devil to see him get a toehold here. His kind, we don't need!"

"It's out of our hands." Will Bonner added, "I'll see you," and left them.

He had one more stop, one he was half reluctant to make.

On a side street near the railroad depot, the restaurant

was neither the largest in Cheyenne nor the fanciest, but it was scrupulously clean and had a good reputation for its plain but well-cooked meals. It boasted a counter with three stools, a half-dozen small tables under red-checked cloths, a high, pressed-tin ceiling, a space heater in its box of cinders for use in the winter months. There were no customers at the moment. The gray-haired woman behind the counter greeted Bonner pleasantly and at his question, "Is Jenny here?" nodded toward the service doors into the kitchen. Will Bonner pulled off his hat as he went back there, still rehearsing what he had come to say.

Operations in the kitchen were momentarily at a standstill, with pots and pans and dishes piled up in the sink—apparently for lack of hot water in the reservoir on the big range. The fire had gone out; an elderly man, husband of the woman at the front counter, stood hovering as Jenny Archer knelt amid a cloud of ashes, with the ash pan on the floor beside her and a small shovel in her hand. She looked around, saw Bonner, and gave him a smile and an exasperated headshake. "This darned stove!" she exclaimed. "When it takes the notion, there's just no getting it to draw! Probably now it's the flue that's stopped up."

"Let me do this, Jenny," the old man insisted. She thanked him, letting him have the shovel as she got to her feet.

She wiped her hands on her apron, came to Bonner, and, quite simply and without affectation, lifted onto her toes to kiss him on the cheek. There was real pleasure in her voice as she said, stepping back, "Will, I never expected to be seeing you this early."

She had a smudge of ashes on her forehead. Bonner touched his own; she used the hem of her apron and he nodded when the smudge was gone. She said, "If you want to wait till we get the fire up again, I can fix you a steak; otherwise, I guess you'll have to settle for a sandwich."

Bonner shook his head. "Afraid I haven't time for either one. I got to be leaving again in a few minutes."

"Oh no!"

"It's my job; I'm sorry. I just had time to come by and tell you, we won't be able to take in that show tonight after all."

"And I was looking forward to it!" But a smile tempered her tone of disappointment. "I know it isn't your fault, though." The old man started working the shaker; above the racket she said, "Let's go where we can talk." She opened the door and Bonner followed her out onto the stoop. Here, facing the blank rear walls of buildings across the alley, they at least had privacy of a kind and they could hear themselves talk.

As he stood in the sun looking at her, Will Bonner was struck as always by the extraordinary fact that he should find favor with this young woman. She seemed to him many cuts above any he was used to being thrown with, in all the cattle towns he'd known from his native Texas to the open ranges of the north. She was something new in his lonely life: a girl of real intelligence and determination, the daughter of a high-flying speculator who, four years ago, had dragged her out to this raw town of Cheyenne, only to die of pneumonia

27

the first winter. With no place and no one to turn to, Jenny Archer had salvaged enough somehow to start her restaurant and, by sheer courage and native business sense, had made a go of it—Jenny herself doing most of the cooking, the elderly Douglas couple helping with the extra chores. But if she was thoroughly practical and level-headed, she was also a handsome woman, still in her mid-twenties, brown-eyed and with a mass of deep brown hair that just reached to Will Bonner's shoulder.

Now she said soberly, "I hope there isn't any trouble. . . ."

"Nothing like that. There's an outfit up from New Mexico. Isely wants me to meet the herd and locate range for it."

"How big a herd?" He told her, and saw her shake her head. "Isn't John Isely ever satisfied? He's already spread over a good part of two territories. I just don't understand what makes men so greedy."

Remembering the talk in Isely's office, Bonner had to speak up for his friend. "Not greed, Jenny. He's an active man, with large ideas. A fellow like John goes into a thing, it just ain't in him to think small—especially when there's all the free range in Wyoming. It's how men do business, in a new territory."

"But is it fair to keep you constantly on the run the way he does, managing it all for him?"

Will Bonner shrugged. "I ain't noticed it hurts me any. He's been a good boss; I've liked working for him." He wasn't ready yet to let himself think Isely had been serious when he talked about leaving the cattle

28

trade, and bringing an end to all they had accomplished in these six years. "Well," he said, "I do have to go. I just hope you aren't mad at me about tonight."

"A little mad at your boss, maybe." But she managed a smile as she said it. They were close, there on the porch in that highly unromantic alleyway; Will Bonner put his hands on her shoulders, and Jenny lifted her face and he kissed her, felt her lips respond.

"See you soon as I can," he promised a little gruffly. He gave her shoulder a squeeze and then, instead of going back through the restaurant, he dropped down the steps. At the building's corner he turned and lifted a hand; she was standing there, looking after him, as he hurried around front where Charlie waited.

Before mounting, Bonner got his gun and holster belt from the saddlebag and buckled them on—it made him feel more comfortable about riding in the company of someone like Vic Spence. The little gunman was waiting for him at the livery, perched on the edge of a water trough with a rawboned bay horse saddled and ready. A cigarette pasted to his lower lip, he gave Bonner a long, heavy-lidded survey that didn't fail to take in the fact he was now wearing iron.

Without dismounting, Bonner said coldly, "I'm not looking forward to this any more than you are. So let's get started, and get it over with. Mount up."

The smaller man gave him a long stare. "You *are* a smarttalking sonofabitch," he said. "But don't think you can give me orders!" Nevertheless, under the weight of the other man's black regard he got down from the trough, dropped his smoke into the water, and went to swing astride his waiting horse. Will Bonner saw no sign of a coil of rope—the certain badge of any genuine cowboy's outfit. On the other hand, there was no missing the stock of the carbine thrust prominently from a scabbard under his right knee.

Stirrup to stirrup, they left the town behind them and the shining twin rails of the Union Pacific. With some thirty miles to travel by nightfall, there was no use pushing the horses; they held to a steady gait that unrolled the miles of trail looping ahead of them, across sun-browned swells of grass. From the rises they were almost never out of sight of trail herds grazing or being worked by mounted riders—an indication of the size of the cattle business in and around this town of Cheyenne. As they rode, such activity thinned out and presently they were alone, except for the sweep of the hot Plains wind, the steady clop of their animals' travel, and the jingling and creaking of their gear.

They rode in silence; neither man seemed concerned with hiding the instant dislike that had sprung into being with the gunman's first arrogant challenge back there on John Isely's veranda.

After a while it suddenly struck Will Bonner that the bay was acting very strangely. It had traveled steadily up to this point, but now it seemed to be developing a tendency to lag behind, as though it could no longer quite keep up with Bonner's sorrel. Charlie didn't like this; he twisted his head about a time or two and even snorted his disgust with the other animal's behavior. Bonner himself, after twice reining in to let the gunman catch up, had a growing suspicion. Finally angry, he backed Charlie in a tight circle, coming around to face Spence directly. The latter pulled up and they sat looking at one another, with the hot wind pressing against them.

A meadowlark let free with a shower of song, out in the grassy sweeps of land.

"You wouldn't be trying to test me, would you?" Bonner suggested. "Maybe you want to find out if I'd be careless enough to let something like you get behind me? Well, I ain't—so you can quit it! The way you're holding us back, we'll be all night!"

"You go to hell!" The gunman stabbed Bonner with a look of pure malice, but after that there was no more trouble. Sourly, Spence kicked his horse even with Bonner's and they rode on as before—in a belligerent silence. The hot day drew out. Shadows grew long, the air turned golden, and the wind strengthened as the sun dipped toward the distant mountains that lay at their right.

Will Bonner knew he could have found the trail herd without a guide; even so, dusk was beginning to blur the shapes of things and the sky overhead turning hard as steel as they came into a break in a low rim and saw the river gleaming below them. Stretched along its near bank, the New Mexico herd grazed, sending up a constant lowing. Campfires, stirred by the chilling wind, made a couple of pools of light with an occasional man-shape moving across them as the trail crew went through the routine of camp supper.

The herd was a big one, all right—as large as Bonner

had ever seen; he had to admit a certain respect for the man who could put it on the trail and bring it, more or less intact, to its destination. Vic Spence seemed to guess at something of his thought, for the man broke his long and sullen silence to observe, looking askance at him, "Ain't every man can do the job Trace Showalt does, mister—and don't you forget it!"

"I always believe in giving credit where it's due," Bonner told him briefly. He added, "I suppose we might as well get down there." He indicated a narrow break in the rim, only wide enough here for a single rider at a time to negotiate. "You can go first," he invited pointedly.

He could almost feel the hard look that sliced at him through the dusk, but without comment Spence booted his animal ahead. Bonner went after him. They made the short drop, and afterward cut directly toward the nearest of the fires.

III

Trace Showalt stood spread-legged near the cookfire, scooping beans and beef stew into his mouth from a tin plate held just under his chin, the wind-whipped flames making a clear picture of the slabby shape of the man. It glinted on the curly whiskers lying close to his jaw, emphasized the high cheekbones and the deep eye sockets and the bulbous nose that must have been smashed in some brawl or other. It picked out a metallic gleam from the heavy buckle of the shell belt around his hips, from the cartridges that studded it and from the backstrap of the gun in his holster. The way the light showed him made it easy for Will Bonner—seated on a stump and nursing a cup of the most scalding hot coffee he'd ever encountered—to see, in this Slash 6 trail boss, the man-breaker he'd heard about from Bud Dorn and from general reputation.

For his part, when he found out who this stranger was, Showalt had shown immediate curiosity. His first gruffly tentative questions soon became more direct and pointed; realizing he was being prodded for information, Bonner made his answers short and nonspecific.

"This fellow Isely," the trail boss said now, his eyes watching Bonner from their shadowed sockets. "I guess he's a pretty big operator, up here in these parts. Sounds that way from what I been told, anyhow."

"He does all right."

"You been with him quite some time, have you?"

"A spell."

Showalt's brows—mouse-colored, like his beard— lowered in a way that showed he recognized the way Bonner was fielding his questions and didn't very much like it. He chewed silently for a time, staring at the other while a gust of wind caught the flames and sent them twisting and leaping and crackling. A fountain of sparks streamed toward the sky that was wholly dark now, and studded with the star pattern of the high Plains.

Bonner returned the look coolly enough. He had no intention of letting this man pump him; John Isely's affairs were none of his damn business. Earlier, Bonner had noticed Showalt and Vic Spence with their heads together, and he didn't doubt but what the little gunman had been passing on everything that happened on the ride down here—Bonner's comments had been a long way from discreet and were probably going to make trouble for him. He didn't particularly care. The more he heard about Rome Patman, and the more he saw of the kind of men Patman chose to have working for him, the less he liked the whole idea of him being John Isely's partner.

Trace Showalt turned up his plate and scraped what was left of its contents into the fire. A brief order, barked at the baldheaded cook, brought the latter over to take the empty plate in exchange for a cup of the steaming coffee. Bonner, who had been working gingerly at it to keep from blistering his tongue, blinked as he saw how the trail boss tossed the stuff down—his throat must be lined with leather.

He put his look again on Will Bonner.

"Fifteen miles, you said, to this Gray's Fork holding ground where you're taking me?" Getting the other's nod, he said brusquely, "Well, we'll get on the trail early, then—I want to wind this up tomorrow." He added pointedly, "We'll just hope it's as good range as you say it is."

"It's the best I got available," Bonner answered briefly, "for a herd the size of this one. Plenty of water, and enough grass that it shouldn't take too many riders to hold them on it. You'll be able to pay off a good part of your crew."

Trace Showalt dismissed the suggestion out of hand. "That's Patman's decision. He may want to keep them on for something else." And he turned and strode away into the darkness, pausing only to drop his tin cup into the wreck pan that sat on the chuck wagon's tail gate.

Will Bonner was left scowling into the coals of the fire, swirling the dregs of coffee in his cup while he thought over that last remark.

Even for a herd this large, Showalt had brought an outsize crew. Most of them, of course, Bonner sized up as ordinary cowpunchers, such as you would see with any trail outfit, or spending their payday money in the saloons of Cheyenne or Dodge—or, for that matter, riding line at one of Isely's scattered camps. But there were the others—two that he'd noticed, men of the same stripe as Vic Spence. These had no discernible chores or responsibilities, as far as the cattle were concerned; they walked about the camp with a certain manner and had been right there when Spence rode in with a stranger: Bonner had seen how they watched like wolves, until it had been made clear just who he was and they could relax their wary vigilance.

They were the men he'd told John Isely they could expect—the ones who helped Showalt keep intact his reputation as a trail driver who never brought a short herd to market. He wondered, a little grimly, what kind of memory they had left behind them during this trek from New Mexico through Colorado Territory. He couldn't help but wonder, too, what new work Rome Patman might have for them, to keep them on his payroll once they arrived at Cheyenne.

Next morning, with the herd strung out like a serpent

across the tawny swells of land, he had his chance to observe Patman's trail boss in action, and the firm efficiency with which he kept his men and his herd under control. Everything was done smoothly, with hardly any need for Showalt to interfere or give a direct order. Almost effortlessly, it seemed, the big drive began the last stretch of its long journey to the holding ground on Gray's Fork, while the sun was still barely swelling above the low horizon to begin pouring its blazing summer heat across the land.

The cattle interested Bonner. While he seemed to check them over, with a stockman's eye for the way they had stood up under the long drive, he was really observing brands. There were a number—two that he recognized at once as Texas, and which seemed to make up the bulk of the herd as far as he was able to judge; others he didn't know at all. On the other hand, he didn't spot any he could identify for certain as a Colorado brand.

If Trace Showalt had been living up to his reputation, of making up his trail losses at the expense of other cattlemen along the route, Will Bonner didn't immediately see the evidence.

He didn't have much opportunity. Since his job now was to guide Showalt to the place assigned the New Mexico herd, he had to take his place beside the trail boss at the front of it. And wherever he rode, he always seemed to find either Spence or another of that sinister trio somewhere within near eyeshot—without any clear duties in connection with the herd, simply staying out of the dust it raised and keeping an eye on the country, and on the one who rode with their boss.

The hours passed uneventfully, one more day in the routine of a well-organized cattle drive. Toward late afternoon, in answer to a query, Bonner reported that Gray's Fork lay perhaps three miles north. Showalt sent a rider with orders for his *segundo,* a grizzled Mexican named Torres, to take charge; he himself spurred ahead with Bonner to get a first look at the holding ground. As though they needed no instructions, Vic Spence and another gunman somehow appeared at their boss's stirrup, and the four lifted their animals to an easy running walk and moved out, quickly dropping the herd behind them in the undulating brown rolls of treeless prairie.

The Gray's Fork camp was as primitive and temporary as most such cattle workings here on the open range of 1874. For lack of timber it had been built of sod, high enough above the creek that a flash flood couldn't wash it out. Enough cottonwood poles had been scared up to shape a corral; just now there were a couple of horses in it. An excavation in the south-facing creekbank, fronted with a wall of timber and sod, gave protection to riding stock during the hard winters.

Entirely too often, such creekbank line camps could be rundown hovels, amid piles of rusted tin cans and a general scatter of trash. Will Bonner saw to it that Isely's camps were kept up in orderly condition—after all, men had to live in them.

Approaching it across the creek, which was shallow with summer's heat, Trace Showalt's bearded features gave no sign of approval. He pulled in and looked around him, put his attention on the sod house with its roof line sagging slightly, and the door and window frames thrown out of line as the walls settled. "Primitive enough," he said curtly.

Will Bonner shrugged. "It serves. It's just a cow camp—we don't have any permanent ranch headquarters up here yet, like the ones you might have seen in Texas. They'll come in time. This is still a new country."

The trail boss hardly seemed to be listening. He had turned his head and was looking off toward the west, where a stain of dust against pale sky told Bonner that Pete Gage, sent out from Cheyenne yesterday, must have been following his orders. Those were Isely cattle yonder, being pushed back up the creek now to make room for the Slash 6 herd. Tomorrow, probably, they would be split up and driven away to the other camps Bonner had indicated, leaving the New Mexico beef to range Gray's Fork by itself.

By this time the arrival of horsemen at the camp must have been noticed; riders were coming at a lope, their hoofbeats echoing against the low creekbank, their shapes blurred against the gleam of sunlight that smeared the dust to gold. They seemed to swell in size as they neared, and presently shaped up as five of Isely's crewmen, with Pete Gage at the head of them.

And then Will Bonner frowned in dark apprehension, as he spotted Bud Dorn's homely, weather-beaten face among the others. He swore silently. He had hoped to avoid a meeting between Dorn and the tough trail boss, but he supposed it had been too much to expect.

38

The newcomers rode up to a halt, the dust they raised dispersed and carried away by a ground wind, as they warily sized up the strangers with Bonner. The latter was already explaining to Trace Showalt, "I told you we'd have to move some of Isely's beef to make room for your herd. These are part of the men who are doing it." And turning to Pete Gage he asked, "Pete, how is it going?"

The veteran puncher answered briefly, "They're mostly gathered; we should be able to start moving them out at first light. For tonight, though, we'll have to count on Showalt's crew to help keep the two from mingling."

Bonner assured him, "They understand that." But when he looked to Showalt for confirmation, he saw that the trail boss was paying him no attention.

Showalt's eyes, set deep above the high cheekbones of his wind-whipped, whiskered face, were a steely blue. Now those eyes focused on Bud Dorn, sitting saddle unobtrusively amid the group of Isely riders. Showalt kicked his mount with one sharp rowel and sent it forward and the others pulled aside for him. Head thrust forward belligerently, he demanded, "What's your name?"

Dorn returned the look squarely. He was a slow-spoken, unaggressive man, but there was a streak of stubbornness in him that Bonner had known, all along, would not let him back away from a showdown with an old enemy. He said now, bluntly, "You know my name."

"I know the face," Showalt corrected him, his lips

barely moving with the words. "And I know there's some reason I should remember it. . . ."

Then the second of the gunmen who accompanied him—a careful-eyed fellow whom Bonner had heard answer to the name of Dunbar—supplied his chief with the answer: "Sure, you remember him, Trace. Two years ago—the Bar X drive. We had to get rid of him, as a troublemaker."

"By God, yes!" Showalt stiffened; recognition honed his stare to brightness as it bored into the Isely hand. "*Now* I place you. I think I told you—whatever your name was—I never wanted to see your face again, around any outfit I happened to be ramrodding!"

"The man works for me, Showalt!"

The sharp retort was stung from Bonner, and it turned the trail boss's head to stab him with a look from those pale eyes. But then Showalt shrugged heavily. "Well, if that's your choice," he said with harsh emphasis. "One that can't stomach the pace of a really tough outfit . . ."

"Wrong!" cried Bud Dorn. "It's only a crooked outfit I don't stomach!"

The words were hardly out of his mouth when the trail boss whipped around at him, fury darkening his cheeks; as quick as the strike of a snake, a gun lifted in Trace Showalt's hand. A shout died in Bonner's throat, and no sound came out; but the man didn't shoot. Before anyone else could have made a move, Showalt was leaning from the saddle and his long arm swept in an arc. The gun barrel struck Bud Dorn along the side of the head, a clubbing blow. Dorn reeled in the saddle, the hat popped from his head; he slowly folded and went sliding off the back of his horse to the ground.

Pete Gage broke free from shock, and swore and made a convulsive clutch for the gun in his own scarred holster. Bonner stopped him by speaking his name sharply; Gage looked at his boss with eyes that seemed blinded by outrage at what they had just witnessed. But warning in Bonner's voice must have got through to him for he held his hand while he looked over at Trace Showalt's followers, and apparently saw that both Spence and Dunbar had their belt guns half drawn from the holsters and were watching their chief for a cue.

It was Showalt who broke the frozen tableau. Holding the gun with which he had felled Dorn, he looked down at the unconscious shape of the puncher and said, to no one in particular, "I don't take that kind of talk!" A pull at the reins backed his horse, then; he placed himself again between his two gunmen, and the look he gave them was all the command they needed. Almost in unison, all three wheeled their mounts and went away from there, at an unhurried pace.

They splashed across the shallow creek and soon vanished, back in the direction of the oncoming herd. But Will Bonner noted that, as long as they were in sight, Trace Showalt still kept his drawn gun on his lap and handled the reins with his free left hand.

Bonner let the breath from his lungs, and looked at his own men. He told Pete Gage, "I'm sorry, Pete. But a pitched battle over a thing like this wouldn't have done any good at all. And we have to remember that, like it or not, those men work for John Isely's new partner."

They were all scowling dangerously, incensed over

41

the brutal clubbing of Bud Dorn. One had already dismounted to look at the hurt puncher. His head jerked and he said harshly, "I think Bud's got a broken jaw!"

Pete Gage swore; they all piled out of their saddles, Bonner finding that he moved a little shakily from the anger that still pumped adrenaline through him. He looked at Gage and the latter gave him a curt, confirming nod. "It's broke. Bud never hurt a living soul!" he exclaimed bitterly, kneeling beside the unconscious man. "And do you mean there ain't a damn thing going to be done about this?"

Bonner met his eyes. "Something's going to be done," he promised. "But we also have to think about Isely."

The other man considered that. He sighed and got to his feet. "All right, Will," he grunted. "I had no business saying that—I should know you better. Besides, what happened is partly my blame. I should of found some way to keep Bud from locking horns with that trail pirate! But, that was Bud—stubborn as a mule, in his own quiet way. He'd never have picked a fight, but he's too proud to seem to hide from one. So he insisted on riding over here with us. I couldn't stop him."

Will Bonner sighed. "I know."

Dorn was beginning to come around. One of the crew had been to the creek to fetch water in his hat, and he held it clumsily while the hurt man took a drink and spilled most of it down his front. Someone else had produced a bottle of whiskey from his saddle pocket and a long drag at this, while the puncher's friends supported him in a sitting position, seemed to help some. Dorn's

42

eyes were still glassy with shock, in a face beginning to swell lopsidedly and already developing a bruise that blotched his entire left cheek. Bonner told them, "If we can get him on his horse, I'll take him in to the doctor."

"Alone?" Pete Gage appeared dubious. "Are you sure you won't need some help? It's a long ten miles—and him with that broken jaw. . . ."

"We'll take it easy." Bonner took the other man's elbow and led him a few steps away, where they could have a quiet and uninterrupted word with the creek lapping and flashing in the sunlight, and grasshoppers snapping in the weeds.

"You're in charge, Pete. If any of the boys have still got stuff in the house, tell them to clear it out before Showalt's crew gets here and takes over the camp. You move up the creek with our stock for the night, and I want you to keep as far out of Showalt's way as possible. That's an order! Above all, I don't want any trouble to come out of what happened to Bud—not here, not now. Is that clear?"

The other nodded soberly. "If anything happens, it won't be my doing."

"Fair enough . . ." Bonner hesitated, then went on more slowly. "I'm not ready to tell the others this, but in the past couple of days I've begun getting a bellyful of this whole deal of Isely's. Of course, you and I, we only work for him. John can do what he pleases; it ain't supposed to be none of our business who he takes for a partner. But, he's still my friend, and this Patman—and the kind of men he hires—well, there's a stink to the whole business that I don't have to like!"

Pete Gage put in darkly, "And there's Bud."

"Yes," Will Bonner agreed. "There's Bud. I guess you and I see things alike. . . . Anyhow, take care!"

IV

It always surprised Will Bonner to see how gentle these tough, hard-fisted cowpunchers could be when one of their own was in trouble. Though their methods were crude, Bud Dorn couldn't have had gentler treatment if he'd been an infant. One of the men sacrificed a clean shirt he fetched from the house, ripping it up and using it for a binding once Pete Gage had gingerly eased the broken jaw back in place. Then, having got a good deal more of the whiskey into him, they placed his hat atop the bandage and among them hoisted him bodily into his saddle.

Bonner again refused all offers to ride the distance to Cheyenne with him and the hurt man. Determined to avoid any conflict between Dorn's friends and the Slash 6 crew, he repeated to them the strict orders he'd given Pete Gage: Under no circumstances was this incident to lead to an open clash.

Afterward, while the others stood mute and concerned, he mounted and took the reins of Dorn's pony, which were handed up to him, and set out on the horse trail that led from the Gray's Fork bottom northward.

He wasn't at all sure that Dorn could stay in the saddle—he couldn't tell if the man was in pain or in shock, or simply half drunk from the booze that had been poured into him. But the puncher had his hands clamped on the horn and his boots slogged deep into the stirrups, and he seemed aware enough to know he had to tough it out, and Bonner held to an easy walk. The slow miles dragged by as the sun dropped down the western sky. Bonner didn't feel like talking, and Bud Dorn seemed not up to the effort.

Presently, where the trail bent to flank the end of a rockstudded ridge, something caused Bonner to look behind him; at once he caught movement far back. He reined in, to study it warily—he could see little cause for anyone else to be using this seldom-traveled trail. There were good-sized boulders here, down off the rim, and considerable scrub growth. Since their horses, at this slow rate of travel, were not likely to have raised much dust, there was a chance the riders coming up behind were not even aware of them. On an impulse, he drew both mounts out of the trail and into cover.

Halting in a small maze of brush and boulders, where the glare and heat of sunlight was held as in a cup, Bonner prepared to wait. He watched a lizard go whisking silently away across the rock where it had been sunning itself when they disturbed it. He listened to the silence, and a thin fluting of warm wind in rock crevices above his head.

Then, against this, other sounds began to grow—a rhythmic thud of hoofs and creak of leather that swelled louder as the riders came on at an easy canter. They passed within a few yards of the hiding place, without breaking gait or giving indication they knew anyone was near. A snatch of talk reached Bonner's ears, though he couldn't make out what was said. Someone laughed coarsely. Then the voices faded.

Bonner kneed Charlie cautiously forward, into a brushy gap between a couple of boulders where he could get a look after the horsemen. There were three of them—Showalt, Spence, and Dunbar; his eyes were hard as he watched them dwindle and vanish, at last, into a swale that dropped them from sight.

Afterward Will Bonner stayed where he was for long minutes, being in no hurry to follow too closely. He supposed the herd had reached bed ground at the Fork on schedule, and been turned over to Torres for settling; now Trace Showalt was heading for Cheyenne, no doubt in order to give Rome Patman a report, and he was taking these two cronies with him. At their rate of travel, they would be arriving hours ahead of Bonner and the hurt Bud Dorn.

That suited him. It gave him no pleasure to hide from someone like Trace Showalt, but with the hurt puncher on his hands he had not really wanted another encounter with any of those men. The simple truth was that he didn't trust himself. His anger at Showalt was a steady seething, which didn't grow any less as time dragged by. For Bud Dorn's sake, he couldn't risk losing his head in some kind of a blowup. Not just now.

He returned to where he had left the other man, among the rocks. Dorn lifted his head and gave Bonner a puzzled look; he evidently wondered where he was, why they had stopped. Bonner tried to reassure him, speaking loudly because he wasn't sure his words penetrated: "It's all right, Bud. We'll be going on now. . . ."

Showalt and the others had long since disappeared. Within another hour this dim trail from Gray's Fork joined the empty stage trace leading directly north to Cheyenne. Still they held to their deliberate gait. The sun left them, in a last golden smear of light upon the horizon, and dusk began to grow out of the hollows. Off the trail Bonner saw the first glow of a herd campfire; he briefly considered halting, but Dorn seemed to be holding up well enough and there were only a few miles yet to cover.

They went on, as night settled and the first stars appeared; presently the lights of Cheyenne made a glow against the darkening sky. "Almost there," he told his companion. "Hang on a little longer."

Lane Morehead was a tall, loose-hung man, with pale skin and heavy-knuckled hands that might have looked more appropriate on a carpenter or a blacksmith than in a doctor's office; but his fingers were deft enough as they examined the badly swollen and discolored features of Bud Dorn. "What happened?" he demanded.

"It was sort of an accident," Bonner told him, not elaborating.

"Looks like a horse kicked him!" Scowling, Morehead considered the problem while the hurt man sat as though only half conscious of what was going on. "Has he been vomiting?"

"No."

"Well, I see no hemorrhaging, or trouble with breathing. It looks like a simple fracture of the lower jaw. In that case there's little enough to be done other

47

than immobilize the jaw and hold it in occlusion till it has time to mend. No real reason for you to worry about him.

"I'll probably keep him here tonight for observation. You're welcome to check back later if you want."

"All right. Give him the best treatment. Whatever the bill comes to, John Isely's good for it." Bonner leaned and put a hand on the puncher's shoulder. "You hear, Bud? You'll be taken care of. Just do whatever the doc says." He wasn't even sure the words registered.

Minutes later he stepped out of the doctor's office into early night that was beginning to wind up as railroad men and cattle outfits hit Cheyenne's saloons. Anger that he had held under iron control was beginning to build again in Will Bonner. He remained cool-headed enough to know that whatever impulse he acted on would have to be carefully guarded; still, as Isely's foreman it was up to him to make a move of some kind. If for no other reason, his continued authority with the men under him depended on it.

But first he mounted Charlie and took Bud Dorn's horse around to the livery, where he turned it over to the night hostler. He kept the sorrel with him, having a cowman's ingrained habit of sticking to the saddle even when in town. Besides, he couldn't tell but what he might need to do some further riding tonight, locating the man he was looking for.

Not knowing where to begin his search, he rode first to the Red Ace on Sixteenth Street and tied Charlie at the hitch pole in front. A kerosene lamp burned beside the slotted doors; as he was crossing the porch, someone in the street saw him by the lamp's yellow glow and hailed him. Bonner turned back, and an Isely puncher named Jay Tobin reined a dusty horse out of the street traffic. He stepped down as Bonner came over to the edge of the walk.

"Damn glad I found you," the man grunted, shoving the hat back from his forehead. "I been pushing hard, all the way in from Fox Creek."

"Something wrong at the creek?"

"Sure looks like it. Looks like that fellow Frank Keenan is asking for some trouble."

He had named a man who, in these past years, had been a persistent thorn in John Isely's hide—a constant challenge to the growth of Isely's cattle interests. Bonner said sharply, "What's Keenan up to now?"

"You know the old soddy that's been standing empty on the upper reaches of the creek?" Bonner nodded impatiently. "Well, he's gone and put some men in there. Nobody had been up that way recent, but today Howie McBee was checking the grass and he seen what's going on. The place has been fixed up some, like they figure to stay. Howie couldn't get close enough to talk—there was three of them around and they had guns, and they yelled at him to keep his distance. But their horses all wore Keenan's brand."

"What about cattle?"

"He never seen any. But I suppose that'll be the next thing."

Which was probably right, Bonner considered, as he scowled at the traffic in the lamplit street. The watershed of Fox Creek had always been a point of rivalry between Isely and his competitor. To the north lay the open range that Frank Keenan used; but it was no secret that he had his eye on Fox Creek, hoping someday for a toehold that he could expand and so crowd John Isely back. There had never been actual bloodshed, but tempers had run high at times and tensions had mounted dangerously. Lately, though, things had been quiet. It seemed strange to Bonner that Keenan should have chosen this moment to start pushing again.

Or—did it? A half-formed thought was already picking at the back of his mind.

"Well, anyway," Jay Tobin finished when the foreman didn't say anything, "Howie sent me in to try and find you. He said I should get word to you right away."

"I'm glad you did," Bonner agreed, nodding a little absently. "Thanks . . ." Abruptly his head lifted and he looked directly at the other man. "Just how good are you at lying?"

Tobin blinked at the question. A grin broke across his sundarkened face. "Never had no complaints."

"Then here's what I want you to do," Bonner said, speaking quickly as he reached his decision. "Go find John Isely and report to him exactly what you've told me—but I don't want you letting on that you saw me at all. Say you were told I'd ridden south to meet a trail outfit, and so you took this news direct to Isely himself. Have you got that straight?"

Jay Tobin looked puzzled but he answered, "I reckon."

"Good! Afterward I'm going to want to know how he

reacts—exactly what he says. I've got my reasons."

"All right. But where will I find you?"

"You eaten yet?" The other shook his head. "Then, when you've seen Isely, go to Jenny Archer's and have her put a meal on my tab. Wait for me till I come—I don't know just how long I'll be."

"Whatever you say." Tobin wasn't one to question orders. He turned to remount the dusty horse that had apparently hurried the twenty miles from Fox Creek. The other stood a moment, frowning over this news he had brought, as the puncher mingled with the traffic and rode away in the direction of the big house on Carey Avenue. Then, with urgent business of his own, Will Bonner turned once more to enter the Red Ace.

Two bartenders were on duty and keeping busy enough, early as it still was. Bonner waited until he caught the eye of the one he wanted to speak to and signaled him over. He shook his head as the man reached for a beer glass.

"I'm looking for someone, Chris," he explained, and described Trace Showalt. "The man hit town earlier this evening—probably would have had a couple others with him. Has he been here?"

"Nobody by that description," Chris answered, shaking his head, which was decorated by a mustache like a pirate's. "Someone as big as that, I think I'd be apt to remember."

"Let's try something else. There's a stranger in Cheyenne these days who goes by the name of Patman. . . ."

The bartender nodded. "*Him* I know—John Isely's

new partner, I understand. But, he wouldn't come around here—this place ain't high-toned enough, according to how I hear he spends his money."

"Where is he most likely to hang out?"

"Why don't you try the hotel bars?" Chris suggested. "If I was looking, I'd start with the fanciest and work down."

Will Bonner nodded. "Good idea. I should have figured that for myself."

He couldn't imagine Rome Patman putting up at any common boardinghouse. But Cheyenne had its full share of opulent hotels, built to cater to the well-heeled followers of the cattle trade, and here Bonner systematically began his search. The third place he tried paid off.

Conscious of worn saddle garb and scuffed boots and a mop of stiff black hair badly in need of trimming, he could hardly have felt more out of place as he walked past a line-up of carriages at the curb and into one of the town's most glittering places of business. The lobby blazed with light from its crystal chandeliers, shining on deep carpets and gold velvet drapes. The desk clerk appeared to have his hands full with paying customers, so it was impossible to ask questions just then or examine the register; while he waited, Bonner drifted over, hat in hand, to take a look across batwing doors into the adjoining hotel barroom.

Will Bonner didn't think he could ever get comfortably drunk in such surroundings. Though the place was well filled, entirely with men, it had a decorous and almost stuffy air about it. No one raised his voice; even

52

the clink of glassware was somehow subdued.

Here were more carpets, more crystal; the bar itself was an elegant piece of architecture—he didn't doubt that important deals, involving many thousands of dollars, must be struck regularly between men resting their elbows there. The mirror behind it bloomed with the reflections of costly liquors sparkling in cut-glass decanters. The two men who presided at the bar, and the waiters who carried drinks to their customers at small tables scattered through the room, all wore white jackets.

And then, as Bonner was about to turn away, the screen of bodies shifted and he had a view down the length of the room, and saw the three who sat at a table in the far corner.

He halted so abruptly that someone entering nearly collided with him and gave him a cursing Will Bonner scarcely heard. The man who sat facing him was Rome Patman himself; at his left was the bodyguard, Morgan Cowley. The third one, on Patman's right—and barely less out of place than Bonner himself, in the same rough clothing that he had worn up the trail from Gray's Fork to Cheyenne—was the trail boss, Trace Showalt.

Though this was just what he had been hoping for, Will Bonner was taken completely by surprise. For a long moment he could only stand and watch the three of them. There were empty glasses in front of them, and they had their elbows on the table and their heads together in what seemed a serious and heavy discussion. As he watched, he saw Patman take out paper and pencil and write something that he showed to Morgan

Cowley; the latter nodded, and Patman returned it to his pocket. And as he did so his glance lifted and seemed to be drawn, as by a magnet, to Will Bonner in the doorway.

As their stares locked, Bonner left his post and started deliberately picking a way forward through the crowd. He came to a stand, looking coldly down at the three.

Bonner saw no one, besides himself and Showalt, who openly wore a gun; but that could be deceptive, because he felt quite certain Morgan Cowley had a weapon somewhere in his clothing—and for all he knew so did Rome Patman. All three gave him back the stares of men who did not welcome this interruption. Patman commented, without warmth, "So—I see you got back. Did you want something?"

Bonner merely looked at him and then, ignoring the question, turned his attention to the man seated at Patman's right. "I been hunting for you," he told Trace Showalt, "all over Cheyenne. It occurred to me the likeliest chance of finding you was to locate the place where your boss hangs out. I figured you'd be together."

Thumbs hooked into belt, one booted leg across the other knee, the trail boss tilted his chair back. The look he placed on Will Bonner was complacent and completely arrogant. "Well, and you found me. If you want to know about the herd, it's been turned out on the Gray's Fork range according to schedule."

"I think," Will Bonner told him, "you and I both know it ain't the herd I'm here about. I'll get right down to cases. I just left Bud Dorn at the doctor's. For your information, Bud has a broken jaw."

"Is that a fact, now?" Showalt sounded only mildly interested, and not at all concerned.

Rome Patman broke in impatiently. "And just who the hell is Bud Dorn?" From this it seemed clear the trail boss hadn't seen fit to mention the gun-clubbing at Gray's Fork; plainly Showalt considered it an incident of no consequence.

He confirmed this now. "Dorn?" he repeated, teetering unconcernedly on the rear legs of his chair. "He's nothing, and nobody—just a troublemaker I had to put in his place." The eyes in their deep sockets returned their stare to Bonner. "But you didn't like it. Is that right?"

"Since Bud is one of my crew," Bonner told him through set lips, "I didn't like it a damn bit."

"The sonofabitch!" Trace Showalt said calmly. "I been thinking I should of busted his skull while I was at it."

Fury seized Will Bonner, like a clenched fist. With hardly a thought for consequences he thrust out his boot, hooked a rung of Trace Showalt's tilted chair, and jerked savagely. Arms suddenly pinwheeling, the trail boss gave a yell and was driven backward. His head struck, an audible thud, shaking the wall so the flame trembled in a bracket lamp above his shoulder. The table went over with a crash.

And as every eye in the room turned, startled by this sudden violence, Will Bonner slid the gun from his holster.

Morgan Cowley, with the nimbleness of a cat, had

leaped to his feet and out of the way when Showalt's blind flailing sent the table toppling against him. A hand darted in under the gap of his coat, but if he was reaching for a weapon he halted the movement at sight of Bonner's long-barreled six-shooter pointed squarely at his chest. "Stand hitched!" Bonner warned him. The bodyguard's ruddy cheeks turned darker but he let his hand fall away, empty.

A glance showed Bonner a couple of the white-jacketed waiters circling toward him through the staring crowd, but when they saw the gun they halted warily enough. As for the customers—well-dressed, soft-handed businessmen and cattle traders for the most part—they looked on in indignation and outrage but showed no signs of interfering. Will Bonner ignored them.

Trace Showalt must have taken a damaging blow when his head hit the wall. He lay now beside his upended chair, groaning and stirring feebly but unable to rise. Looking down at him, Bonner heard Rome Patman say coldly, "You must fancy yourself for a pretty tough fellow."

"I can be when I have to," Will Bonner said.

Patman hadn't moved. He sat with arms folded, head tilted a little to one side as he studied Bonner. And the latter, indicating the fallen trail boss with the muzzle of his gun, told him, "That was in part payment for what happened to Bud Dorn. It would have made Bud feel just a little better if he could see it."

The mouth beneath Patman's black mustache took on a hint of a sneer. "Your friend isn't man enough to settle his own scores?".

"Not when he's laid up, helpless, at the doctor's! Just so there's no misunderstandings, Patman," he added bluntly, "the next time injury comes to a member of my crew because of somebody on your payroll—I'll be holding you directly responsible."

The tawny eyes flickered slightly; then Patman's mouth turned ugly and he said—just loudly enough for it to reach Will Bonner's ears, "You had better watch your step, friend. Once those partnership papers are signed, your days in that job may be over!"

Will Bonner returned the look. He glanced at Morgan Cowley, standing by with his hands hanging empty at his sides. He drew a breath, and slid the revolver back into its holster.

His hand resting on the butt, he swung back to Rome Patman. He told the man flatly, "Hanging onto my job is the last thing I'm concerned about. But John Isely's my friend, as well as being my boss—and what does concern me is the thought of him making a bad mistake. I keep getting this feeling that he could be about to make one!"

He waited but got no answer. Not trusting himself to say anything further, he heeled around and, elbowing his way past a puzzled onlooker, headed directly for the door.

The silence he left behind him broke up as talk resumed. Waiters hurried in to pick up the table and gather the broken glass and right Trace Showalt's chair. During all this Rome Patman sat unmoving, staring after Isely's foreman. On the floor Trace Showalt finally stirred. He rolled over on his back and opened his eyes, to grimace and blink as the flare of the kerosene lamp in its wall bracket struck them. Suddenly he seemed to remember, with a rush, what had happened to him. He let out a roar and started a scramble to his feet.

He ended up clutching the chair to steady himself, a hand clamped against the back of his head. "What did the bastard hit me with?"

"The wall," Patman told him. "Now, sit down. *Sit down!*" he repeated, his voice sharpening with anger. "You fool, the whole room is staring. Isn't it enough they've already watched that half-breed make an idiot of you?"

Showalt glared, but with an angry shrug pulled back the chair and dropped into it, to lean his forearms heavily on the table top. Patman caught the waiter's eye, gave an order that sent him to the bar for a bottle and more glasses. The trail boss scrubbed a palm across his aching head and said, through clenched teeth, "I tell you, I'll kill the sonofabitch. I swear it!"

"It may come to that," Patman agreed. "But for now you've got to walk soft. How the devil am I to sell you to Isely if you go around beating up his men?"

Showalt shrugged again, having no answer for that. The waiter returned with bottle and glasses; Morgan Cowley took them from him and seated himself. As he thumbed the cork and poured drinks around, the bodyguard said dryly, "We have a bigger problem on our hands. This Bonner is the key. I don't know if he's really onto something, or is just suspicious by nature;

58

but if you don't watch out, he can end up queering this whole deal."

"I'll handle Bonner," Patman assured him, irritably, as he picked up his glass.

"You had damn well better," Morgan Cowley said. "Considering the size of the stake we all have in it, you had just better not let anything go sour before we've got Isely's signature on the dotted line. I don't think I have to spell out what I'm saying!"

The look that the other stabbed at him, across the rim of the glass, was almost one of hatred. But without rebuttal, Rome Patman tossed the whiskey down his throat.

V

Remembering Lane Morehead's suggestion, Will Bonner returned directly to the doctor's office to see how it was with the hurt puncher. Morehead showed him into a small room adjoining his office that held a couple of beds for emergency patients. Bud Dorn lay on his back, unmoving, head swathed in a complicated surgical bandage. His eyes were closed, his face bruised and swollen almost beyond recognition. Bonner said gruffly, "He looks dead!"

"Not at all," the young doctor assured him. "He's only resting. In fact, I'd say he's only sleeping off the booze you fellows must have poured into him with a siphon!"

"He isn't too bad hurt, then?"

"Oh no. It was a clean break. If the bone had shattered there might have been internal damage, and then we'd had real trouble. As it is, he didn't even lose a tooth. Come morning, he should be feeling a good deal better."

"Can he be up and around?" Bonner asked.

"Surely. He won't be chewing any steaks for a while, of course; and you'd better not have him topping any bad horses, or doing anything else that might allow that fracture to slip. But if he'll take things easy for a few weeks, he'll be good as new."

Bonner drew a slow breath and let it out again. "That's the best news I've heard in a spell, Doc," he said, and meant it. "Thanks a hell of a lot. . . ."

Reassured about Bud Dorn, he found himself prey to returning doubts about that scene in the hotel barroom. Outside Morehead's office he took his time rolling a cigarette, while he mentally replayed every word and look and unvoiced threat that had passed in those tense, and ultimately violent, moments. He decided he hadn't done a thing he would want unchanged; in fact, there was real satisfaction in remembering the jerk of boot toe that had slammed Trace Showalt's head against the wall and dumped him, dazed and groggy, on the carpet.

But he could have overstepped himself, the free way he'd let himself talk up to Rome Patman—who was, after all, his employer's future partner. He couldn't help being a little appalled at what John Isely might have to say, if he knew; and chances were, every word of that scene would eventually get back to him. Well, it was done. Nothing could be unsaid; and for his own part

Bonner was satisfied that he'd spoken honestly, even if without much tact. He would rather be condemned for saying what he meant than know he'd been insincere.

Thought of Isely reminded him of the word he'd had earlier with the puncher, Jay Tobin. He wondered what Tobin had found out, and remembered he'd asked the man to wait for him at Jenny Archer's restaurant.

He threw away the cigarette butt, and swung again to Charlie's saddle. About time he got over there. . . .

It was late for supper. Besides Jay Tobin, only one customer was still finishing up a meal when Bonner entered the restaurant. Tobin, with a slab of apple pie and an empty coffee cup in front of him, looked relieved. "I was beginning to wonder if you'd really show up," he said, lifting his fork in salute. "I'm trying to get through my third piece of pie!"

Bonner hung up his hat and took the chair opposite; to the gray-haired woman he said, "Bring me anything you got left in the kitchen, Bertha. I know it's late; besides, I'm too hungry to be particular."

She went out. Tobin, without preliminary, began his report. "Well, I saw Isely—give him the word about Frank Keenan, like you told me."

"And what did he say?"

Pushing pie around on his plate with the fork, Tobin frowned and shook his head. "Not much, for a fact. He asked some questions, and he looked pretty mad when I told him about Keenan's men taking over the Fox Creek soddy; but—I dunno, he just didn't react the way I'd of expected. It was sort of like his mind was some-wheres else."

"I see. . . ." Will Bonner was disappointed but, he had to admit, not too surprised—not after the talk, yesterday, in John Isely's den. Isely's thoughts, these days, were definitely not on his cattle business. Even this report of a move by an old adversary apparently wasn't enough to rouse him into action—as Bonner had really believed and hoped, when he sent Jay Tobin to report the news to the old man directly.

Now Jenny Archer came in from the kitchen, bringing a plate of stew and biscuits and a pot of coffee. She said to Will Bonner, "I told Bertha she must be seeing things. When you left yesterday I never thought you'd be back this soon."

Her pleasure at sight of him made him smile in answer. "Sooner than I expected," he agreed. And as she set the food in front of him: "This looks fine."

"More pie?" Jenny asked Tobin.

He almost winced. "No, thanks! Though it's mighty good," he added quickly. "Maybe one more cup of that coffee, to settle what's already down there."

She poured for them both, then set the pot aside and drew herself up a chair. Bonner, commencing to eat, was aware of her look studying his face; she knew him well enough by now that she could undoubtedly tell he was troubled. The room was quiet, street noises entered only dimly. A clock on the wall ticked away the minutes. The other customer got up and left after putting money on the table, and Bertha Douglas came in and started to clear up after him.

Jay Tobin finished his coffee and put down the empty cup. He cleared his throat. "Well, what's the orders?

Howie McBee's waiting up at Fox Creek. Do I tell him we're supposed to pay no mind at all to what Keenan done?"

"No." Bonner had made his decision. "Leave Howie to me—I'll be riding out there myself, come morning; I'll take him his orders. I have another job I want you to do."

"Name it."

"I think you know our camp, south on Gray's Fork? Pete Gage and some of the boys are in process of moving a herd up from there, making room for new stock. I want you to meet them and tell Pete I said he's to take them to Fox Creek—and push it! That beef has got to be on the upper creek by Friday at the latest."

Tobin was staring. "You're calling Frank Keenan's bluff, is that it? You figure to use the herd and *crowd* him back on his own side of the watershed?"

"Something like that," Bonner answered. "If it turns out necessary."

"I just don't know!" The puncher looked frankly worried. "Keenan's tough. He wouldn't have made his play unless he expected to back it up. This could be starting something; shouldn't you have an O.K. first, from Isely?"

Bonner said, "With or without John Isely—either we do something, or let Keenan take whatever he wants without lifting a hand. And after him, maybe somebody else! I never have figured that was what I hired on for."

Tobin apparently read the look on the other's dark face, for he nodded and got abruptly to his feet, taking his hat from the floor beneath his chair. "All right," he said, no longer arguing. "I'll head south, at first light."

"You got a place to sleep tonight?"

"No problem. Thanks for the meal." He looked at Jenny Archer. "Food's always good here, Jenny."

She accepted the compliment with a nod, but her eyes were sober as she watched him move to the door. It closed behind him, and then there was stillness except for the steady ticking of the clock. Bonner returned to his eating, but he could feel the girl's troubled look.

"How bad is it, really?" she asked suddenly.

Bonner pretended not to understand. "Not bad at all," he said, a forkful of stew poised. "I'm enjoying nearly every bite."

"Oh!" She struck him lightly on the arm. "Don't tease!" she begged. "You know what I mean! You and Jay were talking about trouble of some kind with that man Keenan, over use of the grass on Fox Creek. It may be none of my business—but when you ride out there tomorrow, you *know* I'm going to worry."

"Don't," he told her, quickly matching her seriousness. He put down the fork, to meet her brown-eyed look directly. "It's all in the job, and I promise to watch out for my hide. With any kind of luck, no reason the situation has to come to anything like a shooting. Though of course," he added honestly, "there's always that chance, when men go up against each other in a raw country like this one."

"Just what seems to be the problem?"

Will Bonner outlined it for her, as he proceeded to clean up his plate. "It's nothing new, really. There's been rivalry between these two for the past three years or longer—ever since Keenan arrived and saw what John Isely was building for himself. Some men, I guess, just can't bear to be second; and that's the way it's been between Isely and Frank Keenan, both jockeying to see who can run the most head of beef on the largest stretch of open range."

"And own the biggest house on Carey Avenue?"

"That, too," Bonner admitted. "I know you call it greed, but in fact it's simply how the game is played out here in Wyoming."

"Stealing range from one another?" she said with disapproval. "And sending men with guns to hold it? I'm afraid I don't think much of that kind of game!"

"I don't suppose you would—you're a woman, and women have better things to do. But it *is* a kind of game, to men like John and Frank Keenan, and so far the two of them haven't got anyone seriously hurt. They like to push and probe at each other, just to see how far they can go. But whenever it's looked like coming to a showdown, somebody's always backed away."

"And you think it will turn out the same, this time. . . ."

Bonner hesitated over his answer. "Frankly, I ain't sure. There's been a real change in John since he got married, and Keenan may have got wind of it. He may be thinking his chance has come to grab what he wants, and get away with it. The trouble is, thinking that way, he could go too far and let things get out of hand. It may be up to me to keep it from happening."

"How?"

"As for that, I'll just have to play the cards as they fall."

"I see. . . ." She looked so thoughtful that he quickly reached to cover her hand with one of his.

"Now, it's not all that serious," he told her, a smile warming his dark face. "Not yet, anyway. Trouble with Keenan and Isely, they're too much alike—both bull-headed men and stubborn, when it suits them to be. After all these years, I guess I should have learned how to deal with their kind. I don't think I've lost the knack! So, don't worry about it."

He kissed Jenny good night and, as she locked the restaurant door behind him and pulled the shades, went out to free Charlie's reins from the hitch pole. He stood a moment testing the starry evening, feeling the let-down from the day and wondering about tomorrow. When he heard a footstep close at hand, the hurried way he turned was a measure of the state of his nerves.

A figure emerged from the deeper shadows of a store-front awning; Bonner's quick build of tension eased only a little as he recognized the cadaverously lean figure in sack coat and derby—a man of sixty or so, his gaunt face bisected by a sharp blade of a nose. Metal glinted on the lapel of his coat—a town marshal's badge. The coat rode high above the jut of a holstered revolver.

"Hello, Aaron," Will Bonner said carefully. "You looking for me?"

"In a manner of speaking." He thought the lawman's voice sounded mild enough. "I asked, a couple of places. Then it occurred to me I just might run across you here at Jenny's."

"You nearly missed me. I'm heading for the livery, and then a hotel room. It's been a long day."

"Don't want to hold you," Marshal Pleasants assured him. "I'll walk with you a piece."

"Suit yourself."

Bonner started along the outside edge of the sidewalk, trailing Charlie on the reins, and Pleasants fell in beside him. There was no doubt in Bonner's mind that the marshal had some definite matter troubling him, and he thought he knew what it was. He gave the other all the time he needed to bring it into the open.

After an awkward moment's silence, the lawman did. "I understand you had a little trouble this evening. A man named Showalt . . ."

Will Bonner asked bluntly, "Is that an official question? Or a matter of gossip?"

"A little of both," Aaron Pleasants conceded. "The hotel called me in. That new manager from Cleveland gave me to understand he wasn't putting up with any brawling in his bar, like goes on in them railroad dives."

"If he doesn't want brawls," Bonner said, "he should be more particular who hangs out there."

"Showalt, you mean?" The marshal shook his head. "The story I get, the man was behaving himself, drinking quiet enough with one of the regular guests; but then you walked in and picked a row that ended with you throwing furniture around, and laying Showalt unconscious on the floor. Now, Will!" he admonished sternly. "You should know— –"

Bonner halted and turned to face the other; they stood with the night sounds of the town flowing about them on a wind off the sun-baked prairies that surrounded Cheyenne. He said sharply, "I wonder if you happened to ask Trace Showalt—or Rome Patman, his boss—just what that row was about?"

"I did ask. Patman said it was nothing. Trivial, was the word he used."

"We could go to Doc Morehead's office right now," Will Bonner said grimly, "and let you decide for yourself how trivial it was!"

The marshal looked at him. "What do you mean? What's at Morehead's office?"

But the other had already thought better of his outburst, and he shook his head. "Forget it. What happened with Trace Showalt was a personal matter; far as I'm concerned, I hope the law doesn't have to get mixed up in it."

"Well—nobody's filed charges," the marshal said. "If that's what you mean; so at present there's no need for the law to do anything. But I hope you'll take the hint and, next time you got a personal matter, pick a better place to settle it."

Bonner sighed. "All right, Aaron," he agreed. "Next time I'll try. Is that all you wanted?"

"I guess so. Good night, Will."

"Good night. See you around." He led Charlie on down the street, toward the square bulk of the livery stable. Looking after him, Aaron Pleasants rubbed a palm slowly across his lantern jaw.

Half aloud, the marshal murmured slowly, "Now, what do you make of that? Maybe I'm due for a little call at Morehead's office."

VI

Homer Nicholls carried on his legal practice in the rooms where he lived, above a land broker's establishment. It was still early when Will Bonner climbed the outside steps and knocked. He knocked a second time, more loudly; finally the door was opened by the lawyer, shirtless and with his face half covered with lather. Nicholls started to say something irritable about his office hours, plainly stenciled on the glass, but his manner changed when he saw who the caller was.

"Sorry to trouble you, Homer," Bonner told him. "I've got to hit the road shortly but I wanted to see you first."

"It's all right. Come in—come in." Nicholls waved him into the office, adding, "I'll be with you directly." He hurried back to his living quarters while Bonner took a chair beside the desk and looked out over the roofs of Cheyenne, shining in flawless sunlight. He knew this room well—he'd been here often. Outside he'd left the fresh smells of a summer day; here, behind tight-closed windows, were dust and furniture wax and the smell of leather-bound volumes in their glass-fronted case.

After a moment Homer Nicholls was back, having finished shaving but with a daub of lather drying on one ear. He had put on a shirt but no collar. He dropped into the desk chair opposite and frowned at his visitor.

He was a little man with thin, graying hair, and a

manner as pedantic and dry as the prose in his own lawbooks; he had a habit of sucking in his cheeks as he weighed a difficult legal question. He had something of that look about him now, as he adjusted his rimless spectacles.

Actually there could have been no greater contrast between these two men, in personality and background, and yet they had developed a mutual respect during the years both had worked in the interest of their friend John Isely. At the moment, having obeyed the impulse that brought him here, Will Bonner was uncertain how to begin. "First off," he cautioned, "there isn't anything official about this. I don't want us to be John Isely's foreman and his attorney—just a couple of his friends, talking things over. Is that agreed?"

The other nodded guardedly. "Agreed."

"Then, off the record, I'm going to ask you a question and you'll have to decide for yourself whether you want to answer it. As a fellow who knows more about more sides of human nature than I can ever hope to—just what do you think of this partnership John's getting himself into?"

Homer Nicholls stiffened and his head came up. "Any other man who asked me such a question about a client," he said coldly, "I'd throw him out of this office!"

"And you'd be right," Bonner agreed. "What I'm asking is way out of line. But I'm asking it, all the same."

Frowning, the lawyer swore under his breath. He began to drum the desk top with his fingers. "The fact that you want to discuss this deal of Isely's," he said finally, without warmth, "tells me you have some reservations, yourself."

"I don't like a damn thing about it! Most of all, I don't like the change I see in John. Suddenly he doesn't even care about the business we've all put so many years into, and so much hard work."

"Isn't that his affair? A man has a right to change."

"Sure. But I can't believe he's really changed all that much. And I'll hate for him to wake up, one of these days, and know he's tied himself to a partnership he never wanted, and doesn't need."

For a moment he thought he had said too much. The attorney's face seemed to close down and for a long minute they simply stared at each other across the gleaming expanse of the desk. Then, with no expression at all in his face or in his voice, Homer Nicholls said, "Why don't we speak plainly? Is it the idea of a partnership you object to? Or—is it this particular one?"

Will Bonner drew a slow breath, soundlessly, through parted lips. When he spoke again, he chose his words carefully. "Homer, I think you're saying you don't like Rome Patman any more than I do. What does anyone really know about him—what he was doing in New Mexico, where he came from before that, how he got his money? You just don't take on a partner without finding out those things. Besides, I don't cotton to the kind of men this Patman hires."

And he told about Trace Showalt—the tough trail boss's reputation, Bud Dorn's broken jaw, the confrontation last night in the hotel bar. "I won't pretend I didn't get real satisfaction, kicking that chair out from under him," he said. "But the boys were counting on me to do something to help square matters for Bud—and what I did was little enough. It was too much for Patman, though. The thing ended with him telling me, in so many words, that once he and Isely are partners, he intends to see me fired." He added, "I only hope you don't think that's what's eating at me now. Believe me, any time John says for me to go, I will—and no hard feelings."

The other man nodded slowly, as though he understood. He sucked in paper-dry cheeks, frowning over unspoken thoughts. Then, abruptly, he opened a drawer of his desk, took out a sheet of foolscap and slid it across toward Bonner. "You might take a look at that."

Bonner picked it up. There were a few lines of writing, in the lawyer's crabbed backhand, and some doodles and a great deal of blank space. "What is it?" Bonner asked, puzzled.

"The partnership agreement." Nicholls wagged his head at the other's blank look. "After a month of working on it, that's how far I've got drawing it up. If you want to know the truth, I'm stalling! The whole thing is wrong; John Isely is giving away too much and getting back too little."

The foreman stared at him. "Then you do feel the same as me!"

Nicholls shrugged narrow shoulders. "What does it matter what you or I happen to think? John won't even discuss it with me. His mind is made up—and I can't sit on these papers forever."

"But even a day could made a difference—who knows what might change his mind?"

"No use counting on miracles!"

"I thought yesterday one might have happened," Bonner said. "There was news that would really have stirred him up, in the old days. Was a time when all it would have taken was word that Frank Keenan was acting up."

"Keenan, again?" Nicholls made a face. "I swear, I don't know how often those two have locked horns, without anything actually coming of it."

"Well, I saw to it John heard about this. But it doesn't seem to have had any effect at all."

The lawyer spread his hands. "So?"

"Damn it, for John's sake we can't just give up!" With an angry gesture he skimmed the sheet of foolscap across the desk. "How about it—can't that be put back in the drawer? A little longer, anyway? I hear the trout are biting; maybe this could be a good time to go fishing, take yourself a vacation. . . ."

The eyes behind the glasses stabbed him a sharp look. Nicholls shook his head. "No chance," he said shortly. "It's too thin. People know my habits." But he dropped the paper into the drawer and closed it, and after that he swung to his feet and strode restlessly to a window, where he stood peering down into the street as he slapped one hand into the other, behind his back.

He turned suddenly. "I'll tell you what I *could* do," he said, and his tone made Will Bonner raise his head and look at him. "Some business in Omaha has come up that really needs my personal attention. It's a legitimate excuse; I'll go and tend to it. But it also happens I have a case in court, ten days from now—and there's no way at all I can get out of *that*."

"You're giving me ten days—is that it?"

The other nodded. "I'm afraid it's the best I can manage. When I do get back, I already know the pressure that will be on. I'll have no choice then but to get to work and finish drawing up the papers. No chance of putting it off any further."

Bonner drew a breath. "Better than no time at all," he said, and slapped his knees and rose from his chair. "You needn't think I'm not going to take it."

"Very well. In that case"—Nicholls pulled out a turnip watch and squinted at it—"if I'm catching the eastbound I'll have to get busy. There's barely time to pack and get to the depot."

Of the two men in the shadow of a store awning across the street, where they could watch the windows of the lawyer's office, Erd Dunbar showed the strain of impatience—he was humming tunelessly in the back of his throat, starting to pace the dry and rattling sidewalk plankings. Morgan Cowley, by contrast, seemed unaffected by the waiting. The point of a shoulder leaning lazily against a roof prop, he let his pale stare roam the empty morning street with no particular focus or concern. If anything, there was a hint of amused contempt in the tilt of his mouth, as he saw the other's behavior.

"You might as well take it easy," he said. "You won't bring Bonner down those steps any quicker."

Dunbar muttered between clenched teeth. He was a

74

lath-lean figure, careless of his appearance, with a moody irritability that showed in his wedge-shaped face and in every tight-strung movement. There was a danger in him; like the gun in his belt holster, he gave the impression of being ready, at any moment, to unleash violence. He said, "What the hell do you suppose the man is doing up there at this hour? The whole reason for coming early was so as to catch Nicholls by himself and without anybody interrupting."

"Then count it lucky," Cowley suggested dryly, "that it was us saw Bonner going up the steps, and not the other way around. If he'd blundered in on us just as we were putting the screws to Isely's lawyer, there could have been real hell to pay."

The gunman shot him a look. "You that scared of Bonner?"

If it was Cowley's turn to be stung, he showed it by no more than a faint heightening of the ruddiness of his cheeks. He said only, "I'm leery of his influence with John Isely. Until those papers are made out and signed, there's always a chance a word from him to his boss can kill the deal."

"Then why pussyfoot around? There's ways to get rid of the sonofabitch. . . ."

Cowley made no answer to that. Now, floating off the Plains from the direction of the Laramie Hills, the lonesome whistle of a train sounded. Almost as though it had been a signal, the door at the top of the steps across the way opened and Homer Nicholls, dressed for the street, emerged upon the landing; Will Bonner showed behind him. The lawyer carried a bag, which he set

75

down, and, while Bonner waited, used a key to lock the door of the office. He tested it, then picked up his bag again, and both men started down the stairs.

Erd Dunbar grunted, "What's he carrying?"

"A carpetbag, of course," Cowley answered shortly. His tone made the other stare at him.

"What the hell! Does he think he's *leaving?*"

His face gone suddenly dangerous, Morgan Cowley peered without answering at the two across the way, who had paused at the foot of the steps to talk. As they did, there was another wail of sound from the oncoming train, speeding on toward the Cheyenne station; it was close enough by this time that the sound of the train itself could be heard, a pulsing underbeat of rhythm in the stillness.

Will Bonner asked, "Any way I can get in touch with you? Supposing something comes up?"

Morning sun slanted across the lawyer's face, under the brim of his plug hat; he tilted his head to look at the taller man. "I'll be at the Nebraska House in Omaha. You could wire me there."

"All right." They shook hands briefly. The nearing rumble of the train, the whistle beating echoes off the rolling swells of prairie, seemed to act as a prod to Homer Nicholls; tightening his grip on the carpetbag, he said, "I haven't much time. I'd best be going."

The taller man stood and watched him hurry off down the street toward the depot—fairly trotting, clutching his carpetbag with one hand and holding the plug hat on his head with the other. Bonner was thinking, Ten days.

76

. . . It was little enough they were buying, but it was something. The burden was on him, now, to find a way of putting the brief respite of time to use.

At any rate he had learned what he wanted—that John Isely's attorney shared his misgivings about the deal with Patman. It justified his impulse to confer with Homer Nicholls, who was a good man and, in Bonner's estimate, a shrewd one. It was satisfying, at the very least, to know they saw matters the same way. . . .

By this time the train was very close, already beginning to slow for the station, with bell clanging and puffs of smoke from its stack showing above the rooftops along Sixteenth. Cheyenne, despite the early hour, was coming to life; as though from nowhere, people were streaming to converge on the yellow station building—you would have thought they had never seen a train pull in before. Across from Bonner, a pair of men who had been moving at a brisk pace along the shadowed east side of the street all at once broke into a run. Eastbound travelers, he supposed. A couple of drummers, perhaps, delayed over a final drink and suddenly wary of missing their train.

Homer Nicholls was running, too—awkward because of the carpetbag, he cut across Sixteenth heading for the depot's waiting-room entrance. But when he had almost reached it, there was a shout and the lawyer's head jerked about, and Bonner saw him falter.

The pair on yonder shadowed side of the street were hurrying directly toward him; now as they came into the open Bonner got a first good look and recognized them both—Dunbar and Cowley! For just an instant

Homer Nicholls stood and watched them come. Abruptly he swung around and made a lunge for the waiting-room door, but by then the other two were almost at his heels.

As all three disappeared Will Bonner swore and, belatedly, broke into a run himself.

For a man in high-heeled boots, it was a difficult business. The sprawling yellow structure scarcely seemed to get any closer. As he pounded ahead he kept his eye on the dark entrance, apprehensive as to what might be happening in there—whatever Rome Patman's gunmen wanted with the lawyer, he couldn't believe it was for any good. Then he gained the door and he burst through it. A dozen people, scattered with their luggage about the waiting room, turned to stare but he ignored them. He could see none of the men he was looking for. Homer Nicholls wasn't in the line at the window; but then, he would know he could buy his ticket aboard the train, from the conductor. Moving fast, elbowing roughly past anyone in his way, Bonner made his way across the room toward the loading platform beyond.

A station hand came trundling a loaded baggage cart along the platform, to block the exit briefly and hold him up. Then Bonner was through—and there was the motionless train, two coaches, freight and express car and caboose, and the big diamond-stacked engine breathing steam and reeking of oil and heated metal. But still no sign of Homer Nicholls or the pair of gunmen.

He stood a moment, thwarted and baffled. It was for

a moment only. Suddenly a commotion broke out at the door of one of the cars. Homer Nicholls appeared—hatless, pale with fright and indignation, his clothing disarrayed and rimless glasses swaying from their black ribbon. He was still clinging to the carpetbag and cries of outrage broke from him. And there was Erd Dunbar, looming behind the lawyer with a grip on his coat collar, cursing him as he hustled the little man down the steps. Nicholls caught at the grab iron on the side of the coach, but a hard shove tore his fingers loose and sent him stumbling to his hands and knees on the platform. Leaping after him, Dunbar hauled him to his feet.

At this point Morgan Cowley showed, following the others; he had Nicholls' plug hat and he stooped for the fallen carpetbag. With staring faces watching at the windows of both day coaches, Cowley and Dunbar between them hustled their prisoner across the station platform and pushed him up hard against the wall.

The little attorney was game. Strong-armed by his assailants, likely half blind without his glasses, he was sputtering in indignation. "Take your hands off me! You have no right to drag me off a public conveyance! This is kidnapping!"

"You're not going anywhere, mister!" Erd Dunbar told him harshly. "Not Omaha, or anywhere else. You got more important business waiting to be finished right here in your office."

"I'll have you in court!" Homer Nicholls protested, his voice mounting the scale. He looked around wildly. "Somebody—please! Notify the marshal. . . ." Next moment he somehow twisted loose and ducked beneath the arm that imprisoned him. He didn't get far. Dunbar caught him, dragged him back, and cuffed the side of his head with the flat of an open palm. The blow sounded loudly beneath the overhang of the platform; the little attorney's head reeled and his knees started to buckle under him.

Then Will Bonner had reached them.

Fury had him in its grip. He caught a handful of Dunbar's clothing, pulled him around; the gunman stared in surprise and then Bonner's fist struck high on one cheekbone, aiming for the jaw but made a little wild by his own white anger. Sharp pain ran up the cowman's forearm. He saw Dunbar stagger, blinking and gasping, and then catch his footing. Bonner kept after him; when the other managed to fling up both arms he drove through them, ignoring the blow that bounced ineffectively off one shoulder. His own right fist landed squarely, taking the man at the hinge of the jaw, and his left caught Dunbar in the chest and drove a gust of wind from his gaping mouth, and chopped him down.

The gunman dropped to his knees and then on to a sprawl. A little dazedly, he seemed to remember then that he had a gun in his holster. He scrabbled for it, got it out—and the spike heel of Bonner's boot came down hard, pinning his hand and dragging a shout of agony from him. The fingers curled, like the legs of a stepped-on spider. They dropped the gun and Will Bonner removed his boot from Dunbar's hand, quickly gave the weapon a kick that sent it spinning across the platform, to drop into weeds along the right of way.

"Your crowd really seems to favor beating people up," he said harshly, breathing hard from the run. "How do you like it when they dare to fight back?"

He got no answer. As Dunbar clutched his injured hand to his chest, Will Bonner turned away. A glance showed him Homer Nicholls' white and sweating face, one cheek bearing the red mark of the gunman's palm. After that Bonner lifted his head, searching for Morgan Cowley—and saw Patman's bodyguard facing him across the barrel of a revolver.

There was danger in the pale stare that knocked the reckless anger from Bonner like a dash of icy water. The breath caught in his throat. And Cowley said heavily, "I knew I was going to have to finish you, sooner or later!"

Will Bonner had never been closer to death, and he knew it. His mouth had dried out so that it was painfully difficult to speak; but somehow he found his voice, and the only words that might save him: "Go ahead, Cowley. Pull the trigger if you like witnesses. You've got a lot of them."

The warning took effect. Morgan Cowley seemed to surface from whatever depths of killing rage had held him. His head turned, and a quick glance ranged the platform and seemed to take in the people standing frozen, staring at him—the station agent in his alpaca sleeve protectors, the baggage handler, and a half-dozen people waiting to board the train; and, clustered at every window of the coaches, the faces of railroad passengers watching in shocked fascination. Plainly they expected to see this man-for-breakfast town of Cheyenne live up to its reputation before their very eyes.

The gunman seemed to have forgotten them all, but Bonner's reminder stopped him. Even Morgan Cowley would not dare to commit murder in these circumstances, by shooting down an enemy without a gun in his hand. Bonner could see the thought reflected in the man's pale eyes, and in the deepening color of his smooth-shaven cheeks. Cowley's mouth twisted; for his enemy's ears alone, he promised softly, "Don't worry, Indian—there'll be another time."

"Maybe," Will Bonner said.

It was over. The gun disappeared as though by some effortless sleight of hand; the naked hatred vanished and the unruffled smoothness returned. Not even looking at Bonner now, Cowley gave Erd Dunbar an ungentle nudge with his boot and said sharply, "Up! Get up!" Dunbar came to his feet still clutching the wrist of the hand Bonner had stomped. He gave Bonner a long look, filled with pain and hate.

Then Morgan Cowley, with a look of contempt, rammed the man's hat on his head and gave him a shove. They walked away, Dunbar stumbling a little, and the staring people on the platform made way for them.

Bonner turned to Homer Nicholls, who was using a pocket handkerchief to mop his sweating face. "All right, Homer," he said. "Let's get you back on board."

He picked up the lawyer's plug hat and carpetbag,

where Cowley had dropped them, and Nicholls accepted both. Bonner heard him mumbling, in shocked incoherence, "I didn't believe it! I just didn't think they'd do this!" He let the other walk him across the platform to the coach; on the steps he paused a moment as though trying to put a thought into words, but gave it up with a troubled shake of the head. He turned and mounted the steps, and re-entered the coach door from which he'd been forcibly ejected a few minutes earlier.

Bonner stepped back and, deliberately ignoring all the curious eyes that were pinned on him, stood and listened to the conductor's call, the clanging of the bell, the first bursts of steam from the diamond stack. Seconds later a rattle and slam of couplings ran along the length of the cars as the drive wheels fought inertia and brought the train to life.

He turned away, not bothering to watch the train pull out of the station. This had been a bad moment, and it would have repercussions. But for now his thoughts were already ranging ahead to the situation waiting for him at Fox Creek.

VII

He would give John Isely one more chance. Perhaps, after sleeping on it, he might stand ready to be convinced that what happened to his cattle holdings was important to him after all. And so, having seen Homer Nicholls on his way, Bonner got a horse from the livery—a sturdy dun, giving Charlie a well-deserved rest—and rode to the big house on Carey Avenue.

He was undecided whether to say anything to his boss just yet about Bud Dorn's broken jaw, or about this morning's incident at the railroad station. Isely would be upset over both, of course; but as stubbornly determined as he was just now on this partnership, he would all too likely make excuses for Rome Patman and refuse to hold him responsible for any bad thing done by his employees. In fact Bonner had a gut feeling that, whatever he did now, he was going to have to proceed with a great deal of care. Patman held all the high cards. If Will Bonner pushed too hard he could try John Isely's patience, maybe even risk their friendship and the confidence his boss still had in him.

He had reluctantly come to this conclusion as he reined up in front of Isely's house and stepped down to tie his horse.

The front door was open; when he mounted the steps he saw that the Irish girl recently hired by Lavinia to serve as maid and housekeeper was sweeping the front hall. Bonner touched hat brim to her and asked, through the screen, "Would you please tell John I'd like to speak to him?"

She paused, the broom in her hands, long enough to answer shortly, "He ain't here."

"Do you know maybe where I can find him?"

"No." She shook her head again. "Nobody said."

Frowning, he tried to explain: "This is business, and it's pretty important." But she only stared at him. Bonner, who had had doubts as to her intelligence, was ready to turn away in impatience and frustration when a new voice spoke from the living-room archway.

"Bridget? Is something wrong?" Then Lavinia Isely recognized Bonner, waiting outside on the veranda, and she came forward through the shadowed hallway, moving gracefully into the light. She was dressed this morning in cool white that set off the perfection of coiled blond hair and smooth skin. Her smile was the same as always—cool, polite, imperturbable. "Yes, Mr. Bonner?" she said. "You're looking for my husband, I suppose."

He took off his hat as she faced him through the mesh of the screen door. "Yes, ma'am. But the girl says he ain't home."

"I'm afraid that's true."

"Can you say where I might look for him?"

She said, "He's out of town. I understand there's some kind of emergency—at a place called, I believe, Fox Creek; could that be right? I have no idea at all what it was about," she went on, "but he told me he was going to ride out and look into it. He might not be back for a day or two."

Will Bonner found he had to keep a note of elation from his voice. "How long ago did he leave?"

"Oh, I don't really know. An hour, perhaps."

"Thanks."

He was in a much better mood as he hurried back to the street and his waiting horse. For once, something was going as he planned it—some part of his strategy was working! Either Tobin had been mistaken about Isely's lack of interest in the news he brought, or perhaps sleeping on the matter *had* somehow made a difference. For there could only be one reason why Isely was on his way to Fox Creek.

But rising to the saddle and reining away from the iron hitch post, Bonner felt too the responsibility for what he had done. Past confrontations with Frank Keenan had seldom gone beyond sparring for position, never to the point of actual bloodshed; still, there was always a risk. Having maneuvered his old friend into facing personally the threat at Fox Creek, his place was at John Isely's side. And Isely had an hour's start.

Lavinia Isely lingered a moment in the hall, with some further instructions to her maid about the morning's work. Afterward she returned to the living room, saying as she entered, "It was that foreman of John's, looking for him as usual."

Rome Patman had no comment. He stood before the fireplace, studying the oil painting that hung above the mantel—a portrait of Lavinia, done by an artist of some talent, that had managed to catch something of the calm imperturbability of her cornflower-blue eyes, the secret smile that seldom left her lips. And Patman was calmly smoking a cigar, as though unaware or unconcerned about any ban against the use of tobacco in this house outside John Isely's study.

Lavinia stood a moment looking at the broad line of his shoulders. "Do pictures interest you, Mr. Patman?" she said.

"Some do," he admitted, swinging about to face her.

"Though usually not half as much as the originals." He eyed her boldly through the slight mist of cigar smoke.

"Oh?" Lavinia said, and her expression was identical with that of her likeness, which looked down at her across his shoulder.

If he thought he might have gone too far, he showed no sign of it. "Put it like this," he explained blandly. "I'd rather walk through an actual stand of timber than look at the finest landscape ever painted. A picture's dead and done with. But out in nature, every step you take there's a new perspective, to say nothing of sound and movement and the feel of the sun and the wind. No, I'll take nature any day."

Lavinia considered and said, with a delicate lift of a shoulder, "An original point of view, at any rate." She had moved over beside a harp that stood, shining gold and white, upon a raised dais near the archway; she ran a hand gently across the strings and their whispering chime hung for a moment in the quiet of the room. "What about music? Do you care for that at all, Mr. Patman?"

"Well, I liked that piece you played the first evening I came here," he said. "I liked it fine."

"The Beethoven minuet . . . I'll play it for you again, another time."

"It's a deal. I'll hold you to it." He added, "Does your husband enjoy hearing you play?"

"John? Oh, he sits there with the newspaper in his lap and falls asleep!" Lavinia shook her head. "But after all he's no worse than anyone else in this wretched town!

The people here know nothing and care less."

Rome Patman tapped cigar ashes into the cold fireplace. "You have to remember, this is a rough place, and a rough time. It will take a while to knock the corners off. You'll find even Denver isn't really that far ahead of us."

"Don't say that. It will have to be an improvement over Cheyenne!"

"I suppose." Patman was eying her. Despite the discontent in her words and her voice, almost none of this showed in the woman's smooth exterior. He approached her now and she watched him come, without a change of expression even when he stopped before her to put a hand beneath her chin and tilt her head slightly. He looked at her critically, and then at the identical pose of the likeness over the mantel, and nodding he said, "Yes, I was right. The picture's quite definitely second-best."

Bending his head, his fingers still touching her throat, he kissed her.

He was quite deliberate about it, taking his time. Lavinia did not shut her eyes; when he drew back they were watching him, and her manner remained unruffled as she calmly said, "I think it would be a very good idea if you were to go now."

His eyes held hers a long moment, boldly. Then the full mustache lifted, showing his white teeth in a smile. He replaced the cigar in his mouth and, turning, picked up his hat from the table where he had laid it. The woman watched him cross to the archway where he looked at her again, nodded pleasantly, and sauntered off down the hallway leaving her there.

When he entered his hotel, he found Morgan Cowley waiting in one of the lobby's deep leather chairs, a sour look on him. Cowley got at once to his feet; Patman, starting for the bar, caught the jerk of the other's head toward the stairs and changed directions. Mounting after him, Cowley demanded in a growl that he kept low, "Where the hell have you been?"

"Where do you think?"

"I've been waiting long enough. I've got news and it ain't good."

But with that said neither spoke again until they had reached Patman's room and he had unlocked the door with the key from his pocket. The room was a good one, for a town as raw as this—turkey-red carpet and flocked wallpaper, and snowy curtains at the windows. A shining brass bed and a center table holding a lamp with a painted shade dominated the furniture. Having locked the door again, Patman tossed what was left of his cigar out the open window and poured the drink he wanted from a bottle on the commode; only then, with the glass in his hand, did he turn to the other man. "Well?"

Cowley began without preamble. "I took Erd Dunbar with me this morning, to see that lawyer of Isely's and try to build a fire under him."

Patman's head jerked. Angrily he said, "Damn it! I thought I told you to stay away from there! Do you want Nicholls to tell it around that we use threats and strong-arm methods?"

Cowley's ruddy color heightened but he defended

himself. "You know as well as I do, the man's stalling us! Those papers he's supposed to be drawing up should have been ready weeks ago if he wasn't deliberately dragging his feet! Well," he added sourly, "it makes no difference anyhow. He's gone!"

Glass half raised, Patman stared across the rim of it. "Gone! Where?"

"He told us Omaha—business there he suddenly had to attend to. Only he was lying; and for a lawyer, he couldn't lie worth a damn! Any fool could have told, to watch him sweat. Why, he was squealing like a stuck pig when we dragged him off that train—"

At this Rome Patman slowly lowered the glass. His black eyes, above the scowling mouth, were furious. "You didn't! I can't believe you'd think of anything quite so stupid!"

"I sure as hell wasn't going to stand by and let him hold us up like that and not even lift a hand!" Cowley retorted. "Me and Erd reminded him of the business he had waiting to be finished here, before he went anywhere. But then that fellow Bonner—that Indian of Isely's! He got into the thing—he and the lawyer had cooked it up between them, plain enough. With the crowd on the station platform I couldn't afford to have it come to a shooting. I had to let him take the bastard away from us—"

"Christ!" Rome Patman slapped his glass down, hard, and took a turn about the room while he got his anger under control. Confronting the other with fists tight-clenched at his sides, he cried, "Are you trying to kill this deal before I can so much as get it lined up? Manhandling Isely's lawyer in front of witnesses—and before that, Showalt breaking that puncher's jaw! In God's name, how do you expect me to explain such things?"

"Without those papers drawn up and signed, there isn't any deal," Cowley reminded him. "You made a mistake, giving Bonner to understand that he'd be out of a job once it went through; now it's plain that he's set on stopping you, any way he can. Well, with that lawyer out of town, for the time being you're stopped cold."

"Perhaps," Patman conceded as the two faced each other in the quiet of the room. "But then again, perhaps not."

"What do you mean? You got something up your sleeve you ain't told us about?"

"All in good time." Rome Patman brushed the matter aside with the wave of a hand. "Meanwhile, I'll have no more stupid violence making my job even tougher."

"Just one man is making your job tough. That damned Indian!"

"Bonner?" Thoughtfully, Patman nodded. "Sooner or later, we'll get rid of him. But *I'll* give the signal," he added. "And it will have to be done in a way that can't possibly be laid at my door."

Morgan Cowley, with a shrug, turned to pick up the whiskey bottle. "I've got some ideas," he said in rough agreement. "But don't wait too long. The man's dangerous. We can't fool around with him."

The dun was a good traveler and Will Bonner held him to a steady, mile-consuming pace. This was fine

Plains summer weather, the pale sky studded by a flotilla of clouds that swept before the steady wind, tempering the sun's heat; it was as though he rode across a shifting carpet of light and shadow, flowing across rolls of land that began to break up as he headed north and west toward the Laramie Hills.

He had estimated he should reach the camp at Fox Creek sometime after high noon. By pushing—since John Isely was only a fair horseman—he supposed he might even overtake his boss somewhere on the trail, but he saw nothing really to gain in putting that much pressure on the horse, or on himself. And, true to his prediction, when he brought the Fox Creek camp in sight the sun stood almost squarely overhead; and tied to a corral pole, under saddle, he spotted a black horse that looked like Isely's favorite riding animal.

Originally a quarter-section homestead claim, for which Isely had paid someone a good price, this strategic 160 acres was only one of his camps but it served as a main support to his entire operation: for, spread along both banks of the creek, it gave control over a sweep of what was otherwise dry range. It was on such judicious holdings of patented land, sur-rounded by an ocean of unclaimed government grass, that the beef industry in this sparsely settled territory was based.

Given time, as Wyoming filled up, all that would change, but for now there was room for everyone. It was open range that stretched for miles without sign of a fence, barring a few pole work corrals scattered across the empty spaces. Here, a rancher simply turned his herds loose and let drought and heat and blizzards do what they could, feeding cut wild hay in the severest winter. It was a gamble against the elements; the stakes—win or lose—were high enough to give zest to the enterprise, while rivalry with a competitor like Frank Keenan only helped to keep a man on his toes.

At Fox Creek a permanent, all-weather headquarters had been constructed some distance above spring flood level. It was sturdily built, its walls a double thickness of logs and tamped earth between. There were storage sheds, a battery of corrals, a chute for branding. In season as many as a dozen punchers could make this their home base, riding out from here on circle to keep careful watch over several thousand head of cattle, and to man a number of smaller line camps. As Bonner rode up to the house now, a rider named Howie McBee came out on the slab doorstep to greet him.

McBee, a humorless and graying cowpuncher of forty or so, was the man in charge of this camp and of the crew that worked out of it. His manner was somber as he returned the nod Bonner gave him; it reflected the seriousness with which he took the trouble that had developed along the upper reaches of the creek.

"The boss here?"

"Inside," McBee answered. "Having a bait of grub and some talk. You heard what's happened?"

"I heard," Bonner said, and dismounted. McBee followed him in.

Split in two by a partition, with a blanket hung to curtain the doorway between, the cabin contained a bunkroom and a kitchen with a fireplace and long trestle table where the crew took its meals. Four cowhands were there now, the wreckage of dinner in front of them; and seated with them on one of the long benches was John Isely.

It struck Bonner at once that it had been a long time since he saw his boss so relaxed, so thoroughly a man at ease amid congenial surroundings. His pipe was lit and a cloud of smoke hung about him; he looked content and in no hurry to move. He returned his foreman's greeting with a wave of the pipe and made room for him; though he had the manner of someone in a serious discussion with his men, he didn't seem particularly disturbed.

Helping himself to the last leathery steak from the platter, Bonner explained briefly, "I heard from Jay Tobin what was going on. At the house, I learned you'd already come up."

"We've been talking the situation over," his boss said, around the bit of the pipe. "I guess there's no question about it being Keenan's men that have moved in on us."

McBee said from the doorway, "One of the boys checked on them again this morning. Since yesterday they've went and patched up that corral that had about fallen down. Sure looks like they aim to stay."

The rancher scowled. "I'd purely like to know what they think they're up to!"

Bonner sawed at his steak. "It's obvious—they're testing. If Frank can manage a toehold above you on the creek, then he'll start feeding his stock over the watershed as fast as he thinks it's safe. He hopes eventually to chew off a sizable hunk of your range."

"He can't be so dumb as to think I'd let him! The times in the past—"

"That was before," Bonner pointed out. "Maybe he thinks things have changed now. . . ." Which was as much as he could let himself say, without making some unwise reference to the difference made by Isely's marriage. He caught his friend's frowning look and wondered if he, too, was remembering their talk in the den.

If so, Isely didn't acknowledge it. He had been pulling furiously at the pipe; now he took it from his mouth and rapped it against his plate, to dislodge the coals. "Well," he said, bluntly, "if this is a challenge then it has to be met. We might as well be getting at it."

He arose and at once every puncher in the room was on his feet. Isely, stuffing his pipe into a pocket of his jacket, looked around and said quickly, "I won't be needing the bunch of you."

Howie McBee protested, "Aw, hell, John! You don't know *what* you'll be running into."

But Isely firmly shook his head. "If I'd wanted an army, I'd have brought one. I know Frank Keenan; I know how to handle him. You'll come with me, Howie—and Bonner. That should be plenty. The rest of you get on with your jobs."

There were looks of disappointment, but no one argued with the boss. Will Bonner, quickly spearing the last bite of steak and draining the last of his coffee, got

95

up to follow his boss outside. He was thinking that John Isely had not lost the knack of handling crew. It was to be hoped the two of them could take care of this; but not to have asked Howie McBee along, whether needed or not, would have been humiliating for the man in charge of the Fox Creek camp, and it was the kind of mistake in leadership Isely seldom made.

It was why he had always been a good man to work for—and why he had always had the full loyalty and respect of every man who drew his pay.

VIII

No one really knew who had built the old soddy on upper Fox Creek—some lonely trapper or buffalo hunter, probably, who long ago had put it up for a winter camp, used it for a few seasons, and then drifted on. So old that it seemed a part of the land, it was actually a dugout scooped into the face of the creekbank, with a forward extension of sun-baked mud blocks roofed with poles and layers of sod and brush. There was a single door, with steps leading down, and only a couple of very inadequate windows—hardly more than rifle slits. Will Bonner had been inside the thing a couple of times; he could think of nothing more unpleasant than spending any length of time in that spider-infested dark hole sunk into the ground.

Coming along the creek, following its windings as the bank closed in and grew higher, Bonner heard sign of the intruders before the camp itself came into sight.

Someone just ahead was working an ax; the crisp sound of its strokes drifted through the thin growth of willow and cottonwood. Bonner was riding alongside his boss, with Howie McBee bringing up the rear. He lifted a hand quickly in signal to halt and they all drew rein to listen.

"Stay here," Bonner said. "I'll have a look."

He moved forward, at a careful walk, keeping to cover of the timber and letting the soft mud and the runneling of sun-struck water mask any sound of his passage. Whoever was using the ax could only be a matter of yards in front of him. Once, the noise of chopping ceased for a moment and he slipped his gun from the holster, thinking he had been discovered. When the work resumed he sent the dun ahead but kept the revolver ready, resting in his lap.

Abruptly he came in view of the ax handler. Back turned to Bonner, he had felled a small cottonwood and was trimming branches, the blade flashing in the sun and clean white chips flying. He was so close that Bonner could smell the sap oozing from the wood.

He had no hint of anyone's presence until Bonner spoke pleasantly. "Working up some firewood?"

Caught by surprise, the man tried to turn too fast and the weight of the lifted ax head threw him off balance. A boot slipped in mud and he was carried down on one knee. As though too startled to move, he crouched there staring at the rider looming over him.

He wasn't anyone Bonner knew; still, it was impossible to be acquainted with every drifter that moved across the Plains and latched on for a while with one or

97

another of the cattle outfits before moving on again. Unshaven, slovenly dressed, this one didn't look apt to stay in one place for long. Just now he eyed the gun in Bonner's hand as though he wished he could be someplace else—anyplace else.

"Oh, my God!" he said hoarsely.

Bearing down, Will Bonner told him with a cold look, "Since you're on your knees, praying isn't such a bad idea. Especially if you feel like trying anything with that ax!"

Likely the other had forgotten he still had hold of it. He let go as though the handle had suddenly turned red hot, and raised both his arms with hands spread and empty. "I ain't making no trouble, mister!" he promised eagerly. "See, I ain't armed. No gun or nothing."

"Who do you work for?"

"Fellow named Keenan. And I only do what I'm told."

"Right now," Bonner warned him, "you better see you do what *I* tell you. . . . What's your name?"

"Ned Harper."

"All right, Harper. On your feet."

The man scrambled up and stood waiting. "Now, then," Will Bonner told him. "I want some straight answers. How many of you are there?" Turned sullen all at once, the other held back for a moment until Bonner pointedly lifted the revolver. That changed his mind.

"Four," he said gruffly. "Counting Keenan, that is."

"Oh? Frank's here?"

The man shrugged. "He just rode around today to check on how things were going." Eyes narrowing, he suddenly asked a question of his own: "Are you Isely?"

"No," Bonner said. "He is." And a jerk of his head indicated the foremost of the two men who just then came riding into sight through the trees along the creek.

They drew rein, in the dappled shade of cottonwood scrub. Howie McBee explained, "We didn't hear the ax any longer. We had to see what had happened."

Silently they looked the prisoner over; he peered from one grim face to another, and his uneasiness visibly grew. Bonner said briefly by way of introduction, "This is Ned Harper. He rides for Keenan."

Under the silent scrutiny, Ned Harper's courage seemed to falter. He turned to Isely, shouting in scared defiance, "You can't do nothing to me! I happen to know it's public land we're standing on. You own a quarter section further down the crick, and that's all."

There was no change of expression at all in the faces of his captors. Howie McBee commented dryly, "Sounds like a regular bunkhouse lawyer, don't he? For all the good it's going to do him. . . ."

"He says Frank Keenan's around somewhere," Bonner said.

"For a fact?" John Isely echoed. In sudden interest, he lifted reins. "Then let's go have a little chat with him. Better bring that along," he added, indicating the bright-bitted ax lying where Harper had dropped it. "Be a shame to let it lie there and rust. Those things cost money."

"Right you are," said Howie McBee, and gestured to the prisoner. "Hand it up. You won't be cuttin' no more wood today." He accepted the tool as Harper stooped for it and passed it to him, laying it across his lap. With the barrel of his revolver, Will Bonner signaled the prisoner to take the lead while the three riders fell in behind him. Sullenly Ned Harper obeyed.

They left the trees, came up a slight rise from the level of the creek, and then the soddy was in front of them.

Horses stood in the newly mended corral; a man was just taking the saddle off one of them. When he heard riders approaching he took one look, dropped his saddle into the dirt, and headed for the building at a scrambling run. A cowhide hung over the sunken door opening. The man flung himself down the steps, and as the cowhide settled in place behind him the three riders kicked their horses and came in faster, forcing their captive ahead of them.

At first there was no movement about the sod structure; the narrow window slits either side of the doorway remained blankly empty. Then, as the three drew rein with Ned Harper panting from fear and exertion, the door covering was swept briefly aside. Frank Keenan came up the steps into the sunlight, to confront the intruders.

He was a singularly ugly man, with a jaw like a bulldog's and protruding, steely eyes; thinning, sandy hair, turned gray now at the temples, was beginning to recede from a massive forehead that sunlight splotched with freckles. In his right hand he carried a rifle by the action, its muzzle pointed at the ground. He settled himself on wide-spread boots, and looked at each of the horsemen in turn.

Indicating Ned Harper, he demanded, "What are you doing with my rider?"

John Isely said shortly, "Nothing. We just picked him up on the way and brought him along."

"This comes with him," Howie McBee added, and gave the ax a flip and a toss. It spun, flashing sunlight; the bit sank deep into a rotting tree stump.

Harper said quickly, defending himself to his boss, "They come on me by surprise, Mr. Keenan—I swear! I was working and never heard or seen nothing, till I looked around and there was this gun pointed at my head. I thought they was going to kill me!"

"He's full of wind!" John Isely said contemptuously. "We never hurt him."

But Frank Keenan scowled and waggled the rifle barrel against the leg of his jeans. "All the same," he said angrily, "if you got business with me, John, I'd appreciate you taking it up with me directly and leaving my crew alone."

John Isely slanted a pointing finger down at the rival cattleman. "*You're* the one hasn't any business on Fox Creek. We've had that out often enough."

The other shrugged. "Legally, we neither one have any claim to it."

"Who's talking legalities? Until the government closes this range and orders us off, you're sure as hell not going to *push* me off. You've tried before. Did you suppose you'd have better luck this time?"

"Oh, well . . ." Keenan's wide mouth quirked crookedly, in what looked like a cynical smile. "Things change."

At that, Isely's stare turned ice-hard. "Maybe you'd better explain that!" And Will Bonner thought, Here it comes! Suddenly he didn't want Isely probing any deeper; he didn't want to hear the other man saying; It's common knowledge. You've turned soft since you married a woman thirty years younger than you. Why shouldn't I help myself to any part of your range I feel like?

But even as Bonner tried to find the words to steer the talk aside, Isely did it himself. He said bluntly, "I'm giving you ten minutes to take your men, and pull back on your side of the divide."

"I don't think so, John," he was answered, just as bluntly. "Maybe you ain't noticed—but you've got a pair of Winchesters looking at you!"

And it was true. As Keenan spoke, the muzzle of a saddle gun had been thrust through the rifle slit on either side of the door. The men inside had a very narrow range, but they could cover anything directly before the dugout; Bonner saw Isely's head jerk slightly as he realized the situation, and now Keenan was grinning openly at the way he had caught his old adversary off guard.

For a moment no one spoke or moved; there was only the stir of wind through the weeds and grass that had taken root atop the dugout roof, the dimming and brightening of cloud shadow that swept across the face of the sun. Then, glancing past his boss, Will Bonner caught Howie McBee's eye and showed him the yellow coil of hemp he had quietly taken down from its lashing to the saddle horn. He indicated a forward corner of the dugout roof, saw the puncher's puzzled frown—and then his sudden nod of understanding. McBee reached for his own horn string. Bonner gave him time to free the saddle rope; after that, all at once yanking the dun's head around, he kicked the horse into a lunging start as he quickly and deftly shook out a running loop.

Hampered by the narrow range of the rifle slits, neither weapon inside the dugout could cover the suddenness of his move. Frank Keenan gave an angry shout and started to raise the weapon he held; but by this time Howie McBee was in motion. For a crucial instant Keenan found himself utterly confused. Unable to settle on a target, he swung from one to the other as they split away to either side.

Bonner simply ignored him. He had already reached the nearest corner of the dugout and as he went past he dabbed with his loop and caught the end of the short pole that held up this section of the roof. Yonder, at the opposite corner, McBee had missed his first cast but he turned his trained cow pony on a dime, cut back, and this time nailed it. "Now!" Bonner shouted at him. And as though they had been rehearsing, they kicked their horses and threw their weight against the ropes.

Hemp snapped taut, singing with tension. At either end the two short poles supporting the roof timbers took the wrenching and began to give and spring apart. With a creaking and a groaning, the whole weight of sod and brush all at once commenced to sag. Cracks appeared in the roof; dirt spilled through them.

Bonner repeated his shout. Hoofs bunched, muscles

gathered and lunged again. Within the dugout there were sudden, muffled cries. Next moment the cowhide curtain over the door was ripped aside and two punchers came scrambling up the steps and into the open, shouldering Frank Keenan as they fled in panic— and barely in time. One side wall buckled and went over, disintegrating into a spill of logs and sod bricks; the second wall followed suit, almost on the instant, and with that the roof caved in and settled into the dugout with a deafening crash. The dry dust of years billowed high above the shallow hole where, only seconds before, a building of sorts had stood.

As though stunned, for a moment no one moved— no one except Will Bonner, who dropped the end of his saddle rope and reined back to join the group in front of the ruined dugout. Dust was still settling. Bonner had his revolver in his hand and he pointed it at Keenan.

"I'll take the rifle," he said.

All at once there were four prisoners instead of one. The pair from the dugout had come up empty-handed, having dropped their weapons in the frantic haste of escaping. Frank Keenan glowered, as though debating whether to give up his own, but the six-shooter pointed at him gave him no choice. He passed the weapon up, and Bonner took it.

Holstering his pistol, he proceeded to work the lever of the captured gun, jacking the shells out one by one; he tossed the weapon back to its owner then, saying, "I guess this changes things a little." Still scowling, Keenan snatched the rifle out of the air.

He said harshly, "I suppose that was your idea of a smart trick!"

"I notice it worked," John Isely pointed out. "Come to think of it, that dugout was an eyesore on the range and not really safe any longer. A good thing to be rid of it, before somebody got hurt."

One of the men from the dugout was still shaking—a big fellow, named Danny Truitt, with the build and something of the intelligence of an ox. "What about us?" he cried indignantly. "We might have been killed just now!"

"Oh, I thought you could move fast enough," Will Bonner said mildly; and Howie McBee, coiling his rope, added, "The way you come busting out of there, like a badger out of his hole—it was something to watch!"

"All right—all *right!*" Keenan's angry voice sheared across the rest and silenced them. With every eye on him, he gripped the empty rifle and told John Isely, in grudging acceptance, "You won this one, I guess. What do you think you're going to do?"

Their stares locked. If Isely felt any triumph at having once more defeated this rival, he was careful not to let it show. He said, mildly enough, "Why, I guess you're the one that's going to do it, Frank. You'll take these people of yours back where they belong."

It was Harper, the bunkhouse lawyer, who let out a bleat of outrage. Pointing to the pile of rubble that had been a dugout, he cried indignantly, "Damn it, all our gear is down in that mess!"

"You're more than welcome to dig for it," Isely told

him, lifting a shoulder. "Or maybe your boss will make it good."

Frank Keenan looked at the heap of rubble, and at his men. "Get the horses," he ordered sourly, and turned away. And the incident was ended.

IX

Howie McBee said dubiously, "You suppose they'll be back?"

Frowning after the vanished riders, John Isely could only shake his head in puzzlement. "I never supposed we'd be seeing them here in the first place. I just don't understand Frank Keenan!" he admitted. "I never knew him to try anything this foolish. I'd still like to know what got into him!"

If you haven't guessed, Will Bonner thought, it's not likely anyone could explain it!

He had to dismount to free his rope from the timber he'd used it on; now, as he stood coiling the lasso, he told his boss, "Seeing this stretch of the creek wasn't being used must have been too much of a temptation. I've taken steps to fix that. I sent word by Jay Tobin, to the boys who are moving that bunch of cattle we pulled off Gray's Fork, to make room for the New Mexico herd. I gave orders to fetch them here—I thought, with them plugging the hole, it just might discourage Frank from trying this particular trick a second time."

Isely gave him a look and a nod. "Good thinking! When do you expect them?"

Sometime tomorrow. Pete Gage won't be anxious to run the fat off them."

"Then we'll post guard tonight. Just to be sure."

Howie McBee had dismounted and was walking around, picking up odds and ends of trash and heaving them onto the mound of rubble that marked the location of the ruined soddy. "I'm just as pleased to be rid of that," Isely said. "From the way it went, it must have been about ready to fall down. Maybe we'd better have the boys put a torch to whatever will burn." Bonner, fastening the coiled rope to his saddle, nodded.

Mounting, he joined his boss, who had ridden over for a look at the pole corral. Keenan's men had tightened it with rawhide and replaced a couple of missing timbers with shining new poles. Isely leaned from the saddle to give one of the uprights a testing shake, and nodded in approval. "They went and fixed this up real good for us, didn't they? We can always use another holding corral. We'll let it stand."

The sharp-bitted new ax had been left, after all, sticking in the stump where Howie McBee sank it; with thrifty glee he appropriated it, laying it across his saddle swell. There seemed nothing more to be done here and at a word from Isely they started back, leaving stillness hanging over the empty corral and the sunken heap of rubble from the demolished soddy.

As they rode beside the creek through flickering tree shadows, John Isely had some questions about the New Mexico herd. "How did it look? In good shape?"

"Good enough," Bonner said briefly. "A mite trail-gaunted, naturally, but it will fatten on that Gray's Fork grass. I'd have to admit, Showalt seems to know his business on a drive."

Isely had dug out his pipe and was stuffing tobacco into the bowl with a splayed thumb. "I meant to ask you about this Trace Showalt. I'm not forgetting what you said about his reputation. How do you feel now that you've seen him?"

Bonner hesitated. "I'd rather you judged for yourself. He and I didn't get off to much of a start."

"Oh?" The older man's eyes stabbed him with a look. "Maybe you better tell me just what happened."

"All right." Briefly, without dramatics, he told of the scene at Gray's Fork, and the clubbing of Bud Dorn, and saw Isely's look turn grave with concern. "I might as well give you the rest while I'm at it—I don't doubt you'll be hearing. After I got Bud to the doctor, I went hunting for Showalt. I found him with his boss, Patman, and I flattened him. It was mostly for Bud, and for the rest of the boys; but part was for my own satisfaction."

He could tell from the set of Isely's bearded face that his friend was highly displeased. John Isely stared straight ahead, the unlighted pipe clamped between his jaws. Bonner supposed he should go ahead and tell the rest of it—about the encounter this morning with Rome Patman's men on the station platform; but as he read the other's expression his own jaw set firm and he told himself, The hell with it!

If Isely's mind was really as made up as it seemed to be, Bonner suddenly didn't feel like trying to justify himself. Let his boss wait and get Homer Nicholls' story from the attorney's own lips. Whether he wanted to believe it or not, he would have to then.

So Will Bonner let things rest. The remainder of the ride down the creek was made in silence.

Bonner had rather expected his boss would have it in mind to start back to town at once, in order to get there by early dark. He was surprised when Isely showed no inclination that way. They hung around camp as the afternoon waned, discussing range conditions with Howie McBee—the way that water and grass and cattle were shaping up, the possibilities of a late summer drought. When Bonner finally suggested starting for Cheyenne, Isely blandly announced he was staying the night—he wanted to see the beef Pete Gage was bringing in placed on upper Fox Creek before he left.

That settled the matter.

The long summer dusk came down, flooding the land. Weary riders lagged in and stripped gear from their horses and turned them into the corral. A couple of the crew had been ordered up to the site of the run-in with Frank Keenan, on the off chance of a guard being needed there; but an even half-dozen tired and hungry men gathered in the log shack on Fox Creek as buttery lamplight, and a pleasant aroma of frying meat, spread upon the early darkness.

These men treated their boss with respect but not much formality; Isely himself cared little about such things. After they had eaten, somebody produced a jug and a dog-eared pinochle deck and a game was soon

109

going, with John Isely relaxed and at ease in the midst of it—happy with his pipe, with the whiskey, and the companionship of these friendly and noisy men. Once, on stepping out to check the horses in the corral, Bonner stood a moment looking at the squares of lighted windows and at the mesh of stars overhead. And as he listened to the bursts of talk and laughter he could almost imagine a half-dozen years had slipped away—that he and Isely were back at the beginning, before the cattle trade grew from its humble start in creekbank cabins like this one, before Isely became a wealthy man, before the big house on Carey Avenue and the marriage to Lavinia that had changed everything.

Now Will Bonner wondered about his stratagem—whether bringing his old friend out here to a confrontation with Frank Keenan, and a renewed taste of the old days, had been anything more than a waste of time. It had seemed worth trying, a possible way to beat Rome Patman's game by convincing Isely he still cared about the business he'd built and didn't need any partner. Bonner had been that sure he knew his friend better than John Isely knew himself. Now he could only wait and see. . . .

Toward noon next day, the herd from Gray's Fork came spilling over the rim and down into the tight draws at the head of Fox Creek, on schedule.

Isely and Bonner, who had been waiting for them near the ruins of the old sod house, mounted and started to meet Pete Gage as he came splashing across the creek in advance of the herd. Pete's eyes were not as sharp as they used to be and he didn't recognize the two of them in his first glimpse. They saw him pull his saddle gun out of the scabbard and with one accord halted and let him come toward them. When he was within earshot Will Bonner called out, "Take it easy, Pete! It's us. . . ."

Still cautious, the old puncher came on; they saw the surprise in his gaunt face as he finally recognized his two bosses. At once he lowered the carbine and shoved it away, and a moment later came up to them and reined in his blowing horse, his faded eyes squinting from one to the other in the harsh sunlight. His manner was apologetic. "Mr. Isely!" he exclaimed. "Never dreamed I'd see you here! Hell, from what Jay Tobin told me, I was expecting some of Keenan's outfit."

"They've been around," Will Bonner confirmed. "But they pulled out—after we encouraged them a little."

Pete Gage had caught sight, now, of the smoldering remains of the soddy. He stared at it, scratching a leathery jaw with fingernails like yellow horn. "Looks like *something* sure as hell happened!" he grunted; he didn't ask for details. "Anyway, I brung the herd like I was told."

"Good," Isely said. "We'll spread them out and spot them in these pockets along the upper stretch of the creek. The grass will hold them."

A knowing look showed on the puncher's weather-beaten face. He nodded. "And meanwhile they'll help hold *it*—in case Frank Keenan gets any more notions!"

John Isely nodded. "That's the general idea."

"I'll give orders." Gage started to rein back toward

111

the drive, but at a thought he held up a moment longer, his face gone sober. "What about Bud Dorn?" he demanded, looking at Bonner. "We all of us been anxious to know, ever since you took him away with you."

"Bud's in Cheyenne," Bonner assured him. "Morehead's looking after him. He's all right—his jaw will mend."

"And, the sonofabitch that busted it for him?"

Surprisingly enough, it was John Isely who answered. "You mean that fellow Showalt. From what I hear, he got some of his own back. Will Bonner tracked him down, in Cheyenne, and gave it to him in front of a barroom full of witnesses. . . ."

"He did?" The old fellow's face appeared to light up, his mouth spread into a grin. "By damn, I wish I'd been there! Wait till the boys hear!" And he yanked his horse around and kicked it hard, lining out again toward the creek crossing.

John Isely looked at his foreman. "You see, I understand now," he said slowly. "It was something you had to do, if you wanted the respect of the men. Sorry I missed the point at first—I should have figured." Abruptly, not waiting for an answer, he lifted the reins. "Well, maybe we best think about getting home."

With the herd delivered, Pete Gage joined them for the return to Cheyenne.

A blistering Plains wind followed them into town. As they approached the hotel where Rome Patman was registered, a sheet of dust suddenly blew up around them. The setting sun turned it briefly to shimmering gold; then it broke and made them duck their heads to escape its million stinging needles, while their horses balked in protest.

It was Pete Gage, cursing and spitting dirt from between his teeth, who suddenly told the others, "Yonder . . ."

On the hotel veranda, Rome Patman was seated with some of his men—Bonner recognized Trace Showalt, Morgan Cowley, and, perched on the railing with his back against a roof support, the one named Erd Dunbar with whom he'd tangled on the station platform. Patman had a drink sitting on a small table beside his chair and had hastily covered the glass with a palm to keep out the blowing grit. Now he picked it up and was about to drink when he saw the riders; immediately he got to his feet and, carrying the glass, walked out to the veranda steps, hailing his future partner.

"John, when did you get back?" Isely had pulled aside, out of the traffic, and his two companions trailed their horses after him to halt facing Patman. The latter went on, "Mrs. Isely told me, yesterday, she had no idea when we might expect you."

"We just rode in," Isely told him. "A little range matter had to be taken care of."

"So she said." The hot wind scoured the street, plucking at their clothing. Patman raised his half-filled glass in invitation. "Step down and have a drink with us. You must be dry, riding on a day like this one."

Isely made no move to dismount. "Thanks all the same. I ain't got the time just now."

Watching, Will Bonner saw the faintly mocking smile

that crossed Morgan Cowley's ruddy face, and it angered him; Cowley was making no attempt to mask the thought behind the grin—a single night away from home, he was suggesting, and John Isely couldn't bear the delay of getting back as quickly as possible to his handsome young wife. No fool like a middle-aged one. . . .

Isely appeared to miss the look.

Rome Patman had accepted the other's decision with a shrug. "Later, then," he said indifferently, and took a swallow of his drink. Isely was looking beyond him, at the man seated in the chair next to Patman's. Isely's future partner said quickly, "Someone I want you to meet, John. This is Trace Showalt, a man I think can be of use to us. I told you that he was the one brought my herd up from New Mexico."

The trail boss hauled his bulky shape out of the chair and came forward to the railing, to acknowledge the introduction. Isely's returning look was without warmth. "Yes," he said. "And I've heard other things about him."

"Such as?"

"That he's pretty handy, breaking jaws with a six-gun barrel!"

Trace Showalt stiffened. "Any man that needs it," he said, "*any* man—I can damn well oblige him!"

He was looking at Will Bonner, and his undisguised hostility was mirrored in the face of Erd Dunbar, seated on the veranda railing. Bonner merely returned their stares, and heard Rome Patman hastily trying to cover over what had been said. "There's been enough jaws broken!" Patman said. "And enough of this kind of talk.

I apologize for it, John. Also, for that little affair yesterday morning at the depot."

It was Isely's turn to stare. "What affair? Just what would you be talking about?"

"Why . . ." All at once Rome Patman was floundering, his usual glib speech seeming to fail him. He had to see that John Isely was puzzled. He glanced quickly at Will Bonner, and got no help there at all; for the first time it seemed to dawn on him that Bonner actually hadn't told his boss anything about the manhandling of Homer Nicholls.

It did Bonner good to see him blunder into apologizing to his partner, for an offense the latter evidently knew nothing at all about.

Patman at least managed to cover it up, after a fashion: "It wasn't anything much, actually. A couple of my boys got a little rough with one of your townsmen; they were only having some sport with him, but I was afraid if you'd heard about it you might misunderstand. You know how it is when you've had a drink too many. . . ."

Bonner listened to this with a straight face, and so the moment passed. It had had no effect on John Isely. He dismissed the explanation with a shrug and, plainly incurious about hearing more, lifted the reins. "Have to get along now," he said. "Business to attend to. But why don't you drop around at the house after supper?"

"Thanks," Rome Patman said. "I will."

Still holding his glass, he stood watching as the horsemen turned their mounts back into the traffic of the busy street. Will Bonner thought he could feel the

115

special weight of hostile stares, until the group of the veranda had been left behind them.

X

The doctor was out somewhere on a call; the only person in Morehead's reception room was Bud Dorn, sprawled loosely in a chair with a copy of the *Daily Leader* and looking bored and miserable. He showed a look of pleasure and real relief when Bonner and Pete Gage came in; then he caught sight of John Isely and started to blunder to his feet. His boss waved him back. "Don't do that," Isely said. "Stay set, and take it easy."

"That's what the doc keeps telling me," the puncher said. "But I never was much good at doing nothing for too long at a stretch."

"All the same," Isely told him sternly, "those are your orders, and you'll follow them while you're on my payroll."

Dorn sank back, submitting. He looked bad. The whole left side of his face was a livid bruise, and the tight bandage forced him to talk without moving the damaged jaw. Pete Gage asked, in sympathy, "Does it hurt?"

"Some," he admitted. "And I'm already gettin' tired living on soup! But the worst is this damn thing." He indicated the bandage. "All I can think of is one time back home in Missouri—Ma wrapped my head up because I had the mumps, and all the other kids laughed

116

at me. Hell, I can't go out on the street like this!"

"There's no call to feel that way about it," Will Bonner tried to say; but the hurt man only shook his head, and then winced slightly as though he wished he hadn't.

Isely had been frowning as he fiddled with the pipe he'd taken from his pocket. Now he said abruptly, "Will's told me about some earlier trouble you had with this man Showalt. He said you'd made rather serious accusations. . . ."

Dorn looked quickly at the foreman, and the latter nodded. "That's right, Bud. I felt I was obliged to let John know what went on back on the Ellsworth Trail."

The puncher told Isely, "Then I reckon whatever Will said, it was the same as I told him."

"And those charges? Would you be willing to take oath on them?"

Bud Dorn's face was grim. "Boss," he said fiercely, "I never been one to make trouble; I keep my mouth shut when I can—but I know what I seen! Trace Showalt is a damn trail pirate! And now, after this thing he's done to me—for no reason at all—I reckon I owe him. That's the truth!"

"All right." Isely touched him briefly on the shoulder. "Bonner tells me you're honest, and I believe him. Nor do I blame you much for how you feel; in your shoes I'd be pretty mad, myself." He added, "You just stay easy, and do as the doc says. You'll be back in the saddle in no time."

The rancher left, shortly; Bonner followed him outside. Behind them they could hear Pete Gage anxiously

117

asking, "Anything I can do for you?"

Dorn grunted, "You might fetch me a two-inch steak, under onions."

"I'll make that a beer. . . ."

Bonner found his employer standing beside his horse, bearded features dark and troubled. Isely gave him a look.

"See that he takes care of himself, hear?" the rancher told him sternly, and Bonner nodded. He could see that his friend had more to say; he waited, and after a moment it came out: "I'm afraid we've got a problem," Isely said, speaking slowly and reluctantly, "with Trace Showalt. After what I've just seen, I'm convinced I want nothing to do with such a man. Trouble is, Rome Patman seems completely sold on him."

"I noticed that," Bonner said dryly.

"A simple case of bad judgment, no doubt; but the fact remains that he intends to bring Showalt with him when the partnership is formed, and I don't know whether I can change his mind." Isely hesitated before asking, bluntly, "What about you, Will? Can you get along with Showalt?"

Just as bluntly, Bonner answered, "If he comes in, I'll have to go."

"I see. . . ." Plainly troubled, John Isely looked at his hand that held the reins he'd loosened from the tie pole. "I wish you hadn't said that. I'm hoping you'll think about it some more. After all this time, I'd purely hate to lose you. I mean what I'm saying." And so do I, Will Bonner thought grimly—but not aloud.

He couldn't deny his disappointment. These last

118

thirty hours or so, the confrontation at Fox Creek, the reminder of past days—apparently none of it had had any real effect at all. Isely's mind was still made up. The time could be nearing when Bonner would be faced with an unwelcome choice, one that meant walking away and leaving John Isely to a partner who connived with evil and seemed more and more capable of eating him alive. . . .

John Isely said in a gruff tone, "We'll talk more about this. Right now I better be getting home." Home to his wife, and to the mansion on Carey Avenue where he was no longer master of his own house. . . . Will Bonner didn't answer, watching his boss go out to his horse, find stirrup, and lift into the saddle. As Isely booted his animal into motion, there was a step behind Bonner and Pete Gage was there to watch their employer ride away.

Of all the Isely crew, only Pete Gage had been part of this operation from the beginning; he understood his two bosses perfectly, and there was a shrewd concern in the look his faded eyes laid on Will Bonner. "You and John had a row?"

"We could be building to one," Bonner admitted bleakly.

"I don't have to ask what about. Hell, it's clear enough—there's been nothing but trouble since that Patman fellow showed up!" The old puncher hesitated. "You know, I can't help wondering—just what does anybody really know about him?"

"Not much, I guess. Still, out here, who really knows all that much about anyone he deals with? You judge a man by what he gets done. Or, by the trouble he causes."

"That's the truth, I guess. And with a tough like Showalt—and that Morgan Cowley, who's a killer if I ever seen one—" Gage shook his head. "Patman ought to be able to cause plenty!" He added, "How about a drink?"

"Why not?" Will Bonner said, in a heavy tone, "I could use one. . . ."

The Red Ace was filling up for the evening trade, while the heat of the summer day still remained trapped beneath its low ceiling. Lamps were already burning over the bar, which was lined with customers—cowhands for the most part; games were going at some of the tables. There was the tromp of boots, the loud talk of men beginning to feel their drinks. The moment he entered, Bonner had a sharp feeling that eyes were trained on him; yet all he could see, as he and Pete Gage moved down the bar looking for a place, were the backs of heads and the shoulders of men who leaned on the cheap pine counter with bottles and glasses in front of them.

Then, abruptly, he came to a halt. The backbar mirror showed three faces looking out at him with a baleful intensity. They had been studying his own reflection and now, as he paused, the owners of the faces slowly came about to confront him directly. They were the trio who had been with Frank Keenan yesterday, at the soddy on Fox Creek—the ox-like redhead named Danny Truitt, a second one that Bonner didn't happen to know, and Ned Harper, whom Howie McBee had called a bunkhouse lawyer.

Their stares were darkened by a hostility that plainly hadn't eased since yesterday's encounter. Bonner, for his part, had no quarrel with any of the three. He let his glance rest on each in turn, acknowledging their presence; then deliberately he passed by, continuing down the bar alongside Pete Gage. As he did he saw Harper lean closer to Danny Truitt, saw him say something to the big puncher and prod him with an elbow, almost as though goading him. Truitt scowled, not answering.

But Bonner had taken no more than a couple of steps when Truitt was calling after him, in a voice that came out as a bellow, "All right, you! Don't turn your back on me! We'll settle this now."

Will Bonner turned, quite deliberately. Truitt had stepped a pace away from the bar and was facing him with a scowl on his face, his heavy shoulders rolled forward. He wore a gun in a holster, against one slabby leg; it was doubtful whether the big man had any particular skill with it, but at a table near Bonner four poker players suddenly grabbed their cards and scrambled out of range, in a quick scrape of chairs and shuffle of boots. After that silence settled on the room; suddenly no one spoke or moved.

Bonner took a long breath. He wasn't wearing his own gun, never expecting anything like this. With Pete Gage beside him he looked into the ox-like face and said patiently, "There's nothing to settle, Danny. I've got no quarrel with any of you boys." He let a cold look touch Ned Harper. "Don't let yourself get loud-

121

mouthed into making an issue out of a thing that's over and done with."

"It *ain't* done with!" Harper must have sensed that big Truitt was wavering under the other's calm persuasion. "You humiliated all of us—and you could of killed both Shemp and Danny, here, when you pulled that house down on top of them!"

"I doubt that." Bonner let a faint edge of a smile touch his mouth. "I sort of figured them for being able to move fast enough."

"You hear, Danny?" Ned Harper cried, and prodded the big fellow hard. "Now he's laughing at you. You gonna stand for that?"

"I just reckon not!" big Danny Truitt said; his eyes narrowed and his broad shelf of a jaw jutted forward, and his hands lifted and knotted into fists. "I think I ought to bust him. . . ."

At Bonner's side, Pete Gage made an anxious sound and reached for his gun. The foreman caught his wrist. "Stay out of this, Pete," he warned. "It isn't your fight."

"But he'll *kill* you!" the veteran puncher protested, eying the bulging muscles that swelled within the big fellow's sweated shirt.

"Not if I can help it," Bonner said grimly. "Maybe I can talk him out of this. You just keep the other two honest—especially that fellow Harper."

The bartender, taking alarm, had brought up a bung starter from under the counter and was shouting, "We don't want nothing in here. Take it outside!" But he was too late; already Danny Truitt was lunging forward, his big hands reaching. Anxious to avoid them, Bonner

122

faded back fast but a heavy card table caught him and held him up. At the last instant, as the big man closed with him, he twisted aside. The fist that was aimed at his jaw struck him on the left shoulder instead, and instantly his whole arm turned numb.

Even so he managed to raise it, elbow bent, and strike out blindly. He felt the elbow hit home, slowing Truitt long enough for him to set himself and throw a right fist against the side of the thick bull neck. It must have hurt. Truitt fell back a step, with a look of surprise.

Shemp and Harper, at the bar, were yelling the big man on. Will Bonner heard Pete Gage warning the two Keenan riders to stand clear; but even if he managed to keep it a fair fight, Bonner felt a dismal certainty that he hadn't a chance of winning it. Truitt was just too big, too tough, too heavily plated with invulnerable muscle. Let one of those ham-sized fists land squarely, just once, and it would all be over.

He had got clear of the table, but now Truitt was coming at him again with boots pounding the floor and arms swinging. Bonner managed to duck a blow that could have torn an ear from his head, struck back a little desperately, and felt his knuckles smash against the other's thick chest. It drove a grunt from Truitt but in no way stopped him. Bonner backed off. All around him the crowd was yelling even as it cleared out of the way. Their voices bounced off the low ceiling and battered his eardrums.

Suddenly a fist took him on the forehead, just above the eyes. It rocked his head back, sent his hat flying. Stunned, he nearly fell but got his boots untangled. And

123

then a massive hand clamped itself on his arm.

He pulled free, with a convulsive effort; the impetus carried him stumbling across the floor, scattering abandoned chairs in his rush, until he ran full tilt into a battered upright piano against the wall. Amid a jangling discord Will Bonner caught himself, and turned as the shadow of his opponent fell across him. All he could see just then was Truitt's big shape, filling his vision, blocking out the rest of the room. His heavy breathing loud in Bonner's ears, Danny Truitt closed in to finish the fight.

It never happened. A new voice was bellowing angrily, and a hand fell on Truitt's shoulder. The big man swung around ready to strike down whoever had interfered, and Will Bonner took the moment to shake his head, trying to clear it—he was seeing double as a result of that blow to his forehead. Now his vision settled and he saw the face of Frank Keenan and heard Truitt's boss exclaim angrily, "What the hell do you think you're doing?"

The giant's fury had subsided instantly. Suddenly he was stammering, cowed by his employer's anger. "Frank, I'm just fixin' to give it back to this feller for what he done yesterday."

The protruding blue eyes looked at Bonner, and back to the redhead. Scowling, Keenan demanded, "Did *I* say anything about that? Answer me!"

Danny Truitt swallowed. He shook his massive head. "No . . ."

"Anything that may have happened at Fox Creek is for me to settle, not you—not any of the crew. You understand? What put the idea in your head, anyway?"

The big man squirmed, looking uncomfortable. "Why, I dunno, boss. Ned Harper, he was sayin'—"

"I should have figured!" the other cut him off. "Don't listen to Harper, Danny—he's *always* sayin'. He's got a big mouth and he'll do nothin' but get you in trouble." Keenan looked around, seeking out his other crewmen in the line-up staring at them from the bar. "You watch your step, Ned—you hear me?" He waited until he got a grudging nod from the bunkhouse lawyer. After that he cuffed big Truitt on the shoulder and said gruffly, "Now go have a drink and forget it."

The puncher mumbled something but he went off to join his friends; it left Keenan and Bonner confronted. Bonner had his breathing only now under control; his head ached from the weight of Danny Truitt's heavy fist. He looked at Keenan squarely as he said, "I'm hoping all that wasn't just talk. I wouldn't like to think this was your way of getting back at me, and using your hired hands to do it!"

Keenan's face darkened and muscles bulged along the line of his jaw. But whatever angry retort he might have made, instead he simply glowered at Bonner, and then turned his back and strode away. He left the Red Ace as abruptly as he entered. The louvered doors winnowed behind him and the first thickening dusk swallowed him up.

In the streaky light of kerosene lamps, the saloon was settling back to normal; men stared at Will Bonner, their eyes holding a certain new respect for the man who would stand up to Danny Truitt, but they left him alone. And now Pete Gage came over, carrying Bonner's hat, which he had picked up from the floor. It had been tromped on. Bonner punched it back into shape and drew it on after mopping sweat from his brow on a sleeve. He winced a little, thinking he would be lucky not to draw a couple of black eyes as a result of that blow on the forehead. But on the whole he was lucky to be no worse marked than he was.

Gage was full of concern, after the exchange with Frank Keenan. "For a minute," he said, "I thought Frank was gonna hit you, himself! He was *mad!*"

Bonner acknowledged it. "I used him pretty rough. I don't really think he had anything to do with what happened here. But, damn it, I was mad too! A man should control his crew better than that!" He touched a knuckle to his cheekbone, which had been grazed by a wild swing of big Truitt's fist; it had already stopped bleeding.

Pete Gage looked skeptical. "One loud-mouth like that Harper feller," he said, "can make a whole outfit hard to manage." He turned suddenly to look as the three Keenan riders left the saloon—Truitt ducking his head to clear the doorway, Ned Harper swaggering as though to indicate the stern lecture from his employer hadn't embarrassed him. Gage followed after them and said, "I wouldn't rule out more trouble there."

"It's the least of my worries," Bonner said, and hoped he could be as sure as he sounded. They went to the bar for their drinks.

XI

After a few minutes Will Bonner left; Pete Gage remained to buy the beer that had been promised Bud Dorn and then locate a low-stakes poker game for his evening's pleasure. Bonner himself went directly to his hotel room to clean up. His cheek was tender and he was careful of it as he shaved, but aside from that the wavery mirror showed no particular effects from the brief fight—and in that he was lucky, and knew it; those fists of Danny Truitt's might have marked him in ways he'd have carried to the grave. Having washed up and changed his clothing from the hide out, he went down to the street again and walked through the early Cheyenne night to Jenny Archer's.

The restaurant was, as usual, drawing a brisk evening's business; he entered unobtrusively and took a corner table where he sat and watched Jenny moving about and dealing with the trade. Just now she was talking to a prosperous land and cattle dealer named Tom Ryan, a good-looking man of about forty— Bonner knew him only slightly, but had been aware for some time that Ryan was interested in Jenny Archer. He was monopolizing her now, keeping her from her other customers. He managed to make her laugh with something he said, but then Bonner saw him ask her something and saw her shake her head, smiling as she obviously answered "No." Ryan persisted; he caught at her hand but she let him keep it only a moment. She got it back and then, excusing herself, moved on.

Ryan looked disappointed, but not really discouraged. Will Bonner, for his part, would have been more than human not to feel a solid pang of jealousy. He couldn't help contrasting his own saddle-worn exterior with the other man's grooming and tailored suit and polished button shoes. There was no question but what Tom Ryan could have bought and paid for him a couple times over; and that had to make a difference, even to a girl like Jenny.

She saw Bonner now and came immediately to his table; her eyes, scanning his face, were filled with concern. "Will! Are you all right?"

"Shouldn't I be?"

"We heard you'd been in a fight—with a man twice your size!"

Bonner grimaced. "Gossip certainly moves in this town!" he said dryly. "There was a fight of sorts, but it didn't amount to anything."

She said, "I hope not . . ." Still, she couldn't have missed the broken skin on his left cheek. The seriousness didn't leave her, and she added, "Then, too, there was the trouble you rode to see about—with that man Keenan. I've been worrying."

He frowned as he heard the earnest note in her voice. "I'm afraid I've given you quite a lot to worry about," he admitted, "these last few days. I'm sorry—because nothing much came of that, either. I'll tell you about it, but it will take a little time and you've got people waiting."

"Later, then," she said. She took his order and hurried

off; but when she returned with his dinner she told him, as she filled his coffee cup, "Bertha will close up for me this evening. Would you like to come by—say, about nine o'clock? You can walk me home."

Across the room Tom Ryan had hitched about in his chair so that he could watch the two of them, and his well-groomed features wore a discontented scowl. Will Bonner felt suddenly humble. He was certain that the cattle buyer had given Jenny some kind of invitation and been refused; but now she had turned around and made arrangements so that she could have an hour or so with Bonner—a man who owned little more than a horse and a gun and the clothes on his back, and his foreman's wages. He could only accept it as her choice and be grateful for it, though he hardly pretended to understand.

"I'd like that," he told her solemnly. "I'll be here at nine."

He didn't know if it was some nagging thought that stayed to bother him after this brief exchange, or if he was still feeling the punishment he'd taken from Truitt's bruising fists; whatever the reason, Will Bonner was troubled by a feeling of letdown that he seemed unable to shake. Now, with an hour to kill before returning for Jenny, he decided he didn't want to spend the time in a saloon so he started back to the hotel, absorbed in his own mood and not too aware of the life around him in Cheyenne's nighttime, lamp-splashed streets.

When he halted at a corner, to let a wagon creak past,

he failed to sense someone behind him until he heard a movement and felt a gun's muzzle thrust suddenly against the meat of his back. A voice that he knew told him, in a flat monotone that held more threat than any shout, "Don't make trouble. Just turn left and keep walking till I say stop."

With the weapon rammed against him and his own six-gun left behind at the hotel, he knew better than to try resisting. Still, it wasn't pleasant to admit he'd let himself be taken by surprise; this made him slow to accept what was happening to him, and as he hesitated the voice took on a warning sharpness: "I said, don't give me any trouble. I mean it! You better believe I'd as soon drill you as not, Bonner!"

He turned his head, then, and looked at Vic Spence. A stray gleam of lamplight struck the face of the little gunman and glittered in his eyes. There could be no question of his bluffing about using the gun. He rammed it harder, motioning with his head in the direction he wanted his prisoner to go. Will Bonner shrugged, and gave to the gun's prodding.

The side street was poorly lighted and the sidewalk, just now, nearly empty. Bonner walked carefully, always conscious of those other footsteps just behind him on the uneven wooden plankings; he kept his hands well in sight, knowing the taut spring Vic Spence held himself on—any suspicious move could be fatal. Only once did he venture a question: "Are you following orders? Or is this your own idea?"

"Don't worry about that!" the gunman retorted. "You just walk."

Half a block farther, he called a halt in front of a narrow frame building whose lower floor, according to lettering dimly visible on darkened plate glass, housed a title and abstract company. There was lamplight in second-story windows, and a doorway opening onto narrow, uncarpeted stairs with the dim glow of a single lamp showing at their top. "Up you go," Vic Spence said roughly.

They climbed, Bonner still in front and their boots sending cavernous echoes chasing up the stairwell. But now the gun's muzzle was no longer jammed against the prisoner's back, and pride, if nothing else, dictated that he at least try to take advantage of it.

They were halfway to the top when, as though by accident, Bonner let his boot slip off the edge of the next step. It threw him forward into a stumble, catching his weight on his hands as the hard edge of a step struck him painfully across the chest; every muscle tensed against the smash of a bullet, he drove a boot behind him as hard as he could kick.

He felt it strike resistance; twisting, he looked across his shoulder and saw Spence tottering, driven off balance. The little gunman's head went back, his arms windmilled. He lost his revolver and after that he was toppling, and his cry filled the stairwell. He went head-first down the stairs with the gun clattering after him.

Bonner winced painfully as his eyes followed the other down; a fall like that could easily break a man's neck. Spence made a complete backward somersault and was brought up motionless at the bottom of the steps, head canted at an angle against the wall—it was impossible to tell if he was badly injured or only stunned. Will Bonner let out the breath he'd been holding, and got his boots under him. A door at the top of the stairwell had swung open. He looked up and froze as he saw Morgan Cowley staring down—and saw the gun pointed squarely at his face.

Rome Patman's bodyguard came to the edge of the steps for a look at Vic Spence's sprawled shape, and then gave Bonner a wicked grin. "So he got careless, did he? We warned him you'd prove a handful if he gave you half a chance. How bad is he damaged?"

For answer a groan broke from Spence and the man began to stir, moving groggily and seemingly only half conscious. Cowley watched him struggle to a sitting position, and dismissed the problem. "He'll live. . . . All right, Bonner—come on up. We've been waiting for you."

The prisoner shrugged. With the muzzle of Cowley's revolver trained on him, like a third eye carefully watching every move, he climbed the steps and, at the top, halted while Cowley pushed his coat back to make sure he had no weapon on him. Motioned toward the open door, Bonner went past the gunman and halted on the threshold.

The place was an office. There was a flat desk with a shining top, a straight chair beside it, a couple more against the wall. A wooden file cabinet filled one corner, and another held a small iron box safe. Everything looked new. The air was heavy with a smell of furniture polish and fresh paint.

Seated comfortably in a barrel chair behind the desk,

hands laced across his chest, Rome Patman looked at the man in the doorway. The glow of a wall lamp behind him cast odd shadows over his face, and his eyes peered out of this expressionless mask; he tilted his head in a mocking gesture of greeting. "No need to be formal," he said pleasantly. "Just walk in."

A sharp nudge from behind made the invitation a command, and Will Bonner did as he was told. Having watched his inventory of the room, Patman said, "First time you've been up here. I just moved in. A man in business needs a base of operations."

"It's not bad," Bonner said dryly.

Patman waved a hand toward the straight chair across from him. "Have a seat. And we'll talk."

At that moment there was an eruption of sound outside the office as someone came storming up the stairs. Morgan Cowley was just closing the door when it was violently shoved open and Vic Spence burst in. The little gunman looked wild. There was blood on his face and his stare searched the room. It settled on Bonner, and, brandishing the gun he'd recovered on his way up, Spence gave a wordless cry of rage and leaped straight at him.

Bonner thoroughly expected to be shot down where he stood. But Morgan Cowley was a quick-moving man; he stepped and seized Spence by an arm and easily hauled him back, while a further twist at the arm made the gunman open his fist and let the gun fall at his feet. Released, Spence glared about him, almost incoherent in his plain fury and frustration.

Cowley said crisply, "Just cool down."

"You didn't *see!*" Spittle flew from the corners of the little gunman's mouth. "You don't know what this bastard did!"

"He dumped you," Cowley said. "He threw your butt down the stairs. If you'd paid attention to what you were doing it wouldn't have happened—so quit fussing."

"No, by God! He could have broken my neck!"

Rome Patman had not changed position in the comfortable chair behind his desk. Without raising his voice, he simply spoke the gunman's name. Spence jerked around, and at what he saw in Patman's face something appeared to go out of him. He subsided, though sullen and scowling, as in the same unruffled tone his boss told him, "You had your orders. You were supposed to bring him here, but nothing was said about getting rough. You don't listen very well, Spence." And with that, a nod toward the door dismissed the man.

Vic Spence gave Bonner a last look, and Bonner read pure hatred in it. Bonner forced himself to meet it, knowing it was his keen susceptibility to humiliation that could make a man as small as Spence really dangerous. Whatever was in his mind he let the look say it all; sleeving blood from his face, he turned and stomped out. At the door Morgan Cowley offered him his gun. Spence snatched it from his hand and was gone, tromping down the steps. Cowley closed the door behind him.

It had been no more than an interruption. As though nothing at all had happened, Rome Patman again indicated the chair and Bonner slacked into it, without removing his hat. Patman had opened the lid of a cigar box and, having selected one for himself, pushed the box across the desk top in Bonner's direction. More puzzled than ever at what he was doing here, he accepted the offer and also a match from a container on the desk. They lighted up their smokes, no one speaking until the ritual was completed. Cowley remained where he was, leaning his shoulders against the wall beside the closed door.

Patman examined the burning end of his cigar, settled back, and blew smoke at the ceiling. His glance sought Bonner's face. "A fellow like Spence," he pointed out, "you have to give him his head. But then, sometimes he has to be hauled up short."

"Just keep him away from me," Bonner said. "After tonight, one of us might have to end up killing the other—and I don't intend to be easy to kill!"

"Don't underestimate Vic Spence," the other warned, but Bonner merely shrugged and changed the subject.

"Maybe you'll tell me, now, why I was brought up here. It wasn't just to show me your office—or have me sample your cigars. You and me ain't on those terms."

"No," Patman agreed. "And frankly, that's what has me puzzled. I'll ask you point-blank—with no one but us to hear the answer. How is it John Isely didn't know about that little mistake my boys made yesterday morning at the depot? Let's be frank," he went on, when Bonner only returned his look without answering, "getting rough with Isely's attorney was a really stupid business. There was no excuse for it at all, and ever since I heard about it I've looked forward to a hard time trying to make a plausible explanation. Then it turns out that he was never even told. Why?"

Bonner could have answered truthfully: Because the story will make a bigger impression on him coming from Homer Nicholls than if *I* tried to tell him! But instead he said, briefly, "I had my reasons."

"I'm sure of that!" Blue smoke came out with the words, forming a screen before Patman's face. He batted it away with the hand that held the cigar, his eyes still pinned thoughtfully on the other man. "But it doesn't square! I take you for a pretty smart fellow, Bonner," he went on. "Smart enough to admit it when you see you aren't going to win—and, you aren't going to win this time! Sneaking that lawyer out of town, so he couldn't finish drawing up the papers—it was a clever delaying move, but nothing more than that. Believe me! Isely is dead set on this partnership and he's not going to be changing his mind. And however much you fight the idea, I think you know it's the truth."

Will Bonner, meeting his look across the polished desk top, began to be aware of a bitter taste in his mouth. Rome Patman wasn't boasting, and he wasn't talking just to hear himself. He was laying out cold facts, and the other had to admit it.

"And so," Patman continued when he saw Bonner wasn't going to offer any comment, "ever since it became clear this evening that you hadn't tried to queer my play with John Isely, by reporting what happened to the lawyer, I've been asking myself what could have been your reason. You can correct me if

I'm wrong; but I think now I know."

"Do you?"

"I think you're signaling that you might be ready to talk a deal."

The words hung heavy in the stillness. After a moment Bonner drew a slow breath and said carefully, "Now that you brought it up, what's your idea of a deal?"

"Oh, I can be generous." Patman was obviously in a good humor. "You've had a very nice thing here; no one could blame you for hating to see it all go. As a matter of fact, if you'd only look at things sensibly I'd be in favor of you staying on, awhile at least. But somehow I get a feeling you wouldn't want to work for me, under any circumstances."

Tight-lipped, Bonner said, "You've called that straight enough!"

The black eyes considered him, as Patman ran a finger across the thick mustache. "Suppose *you* put a figure on it, then," he suggested. "What's your price, to stop bucking me at every turn and, instead, do whatever you can to help move this thing along? Remember— when you leave it could mean the difference between walking away empty-handed, or with a stake toward setting up somewhere else. And if what I hear is true, that could be pretty important." A corner of his mouth quirked slightly. "There's a young woman, I under-stand—and, I might add, a very handsome one. I've taken a few meals at her restaurant, just for the purpose of getting a look at her."

Will Bonner could feel the heat rising in his face.

Stung, he exclaimed, "You don't miss much, do you?"

"Never, where my interests are concerned. . . . Well? What do you say?"

Bonner took his time deliberately stubbing out his cigar in the ashtray on the desk. Then he lifted his glance squarely at the other man. "What I say," he answered coldly, "is that you can go straight to hell!"

There was a sound from Morgan Cowley, over by the door. Bonner didn't look at him. Suddenly he was on his feet, booting back his chair; more slowly, Patman rose to face him. Patman's features had settled into a mask that showed nothing as Bonner plunged ahead, suddenly too angry to hold back.

"I still haven't figured your game—not completely. But if I ever needed proof it was crooked, you've just given it to me. This bribe offer convinces me more than ever that, whatever comes of the partnership, it can't mean any good for John Isely!"

Patman's black eyes bored into him. He said bluntly, "Take the offer now, or you'll never have another chance."

"All you'll get from me," Bonner promised grimly, "is a fight—right to the end!"

He was breathing hard when he finished and his hands were trembling, but he had the satisfaction of seeing that he had somehow got past the other man's cool front, and stung a faint flush of color into his cheeks. But Patman's voice held level as, shaking his head, he said, "I guess I was wrong about you, after all. I certainly never took you for a fool, or I wouldn't have gone to the bother of bringing you up here."

"Well, here I am!" Bonner snapped. He looked at Morgan Cowley. "I've got no gun on me. I suppose the two of you can finish this right now, if you want to."

Cowley seemed ready enough. Rome Patman, however, merely shook his head again. "*I'm* not a fool," he said. "This isn't the place, or the time." He glanced at his bodyguard. "Let him go."

The blond gunman scowled, as though he disagreed; but without arguing he shrugged and, stepping to the door, swung it wide. "You're in luck this time, Indian," he said sharply. "Go ahead."

Bonner's eyes narrowed. "You keep calling me that, Cowley—like you thought it was an insult. So far as I know I haven't got any Indian in me; but I'd be just as pleased to admit it, when I see your kind of white man!" He looked again at Patman, who was watching him from behind the desk, waiting for him to go. Everything in Bonner rebelled at being dismissed this way, with a contemptuous gesture, but at the moment he had no choice. He started abruptly for the door but as he reached it he was stopped for an instant by a final word from Patman.

"You're licked, Bonner," the man said with cold certainty. "Don't let yourself think otherwise, not for a minute. I know what I want—and you'll never stop me."

The other returned his look—the bars down between them, the naked enmity showing. "Maybe," Will Bonner said then, curtly. "We'll see."

He walked out of the room and down the stairs, and his boots echoed hollowly on the uncarpeted treads.

XII

The restaurant was closed by the time Bonner got back there, the last customer gone; Jenny Archer had on her hat and coat and was waiting, chatting with Mrs. Douglas as the older woman scrubbed down the tables in the dining room. Bonner took the girl's arm, and when they stepped out into the night he heard her sigh and sensed the slight but definite sag of her shoulders. Behind them the lock clicked as Mrs. Douglas turned the key.

"Tired?" Bonner asked, sympathetically.

"Exhausted. It's been an endless sort of day." She added quickly, "But I'm young, a little hard work can't hurt me any. What *does* bother me is to watch the Douglases—such long hours they put in, and at their time of life! I don't know how they manage. It makes me feel guilty, not being able at least to pay them better."

"You give them security," he pointed out. "It's worth having, at their age." But something in her words oppressed him and turned him silent, and as they moved on along the shadowed street there was only the slur of their own footsteps, the heat of the spent day still radiating from timbers that had soaked up the sun, the acrid smell of dust lying thick in the street ruts.

Presently Jenny said, with a little laugh, "We're not very talkative tonight, are we?"

He literally shook himself out of the mood that had settled on him. "I'm sorry! I guess I promised to fill you in on what happened out at Fox Creek. But, actually, there isn't all that much to tell. As I'd expected, we ran into some talk and bluster; but Keenan knew he'd over-reached himself. There was only one way it could end—he had to pull in his horns for the time being."

"And that's all there was to it?" And when he nodded: "But what about the fight this evening?"

"Oh, that was just one of Frank Keenan's boys who didn't like the way things turned out, and didn't want to let it stop there. Actually, Keenan broke it up. Nobody got hurt." His head still ached dully from that clubbing blow of Danny Truitt's he'd taken between the eyes, but he had no intention of letting her know.

They walked in silence, her hand tucked into Bonner's arm, her thoughts plainly concerned with what he had told her. "So what happens now?"

"Probably nothing. At least not right away. Keenan's had his fingers burned; he'll have to back off and think it over. Like I told you—it's a kind of game."

Turning a corner, they stopped before a small white frame house enclosed by a picket fence—he knew Jenny Archer tried to keep the fence and the house in good repair, but the hot Plains winds and blistering summer sun took their toll of the best paint job. Cottonwoods rattled their dry leaves overhead, letting down a shifting film of moonlight that touched the girl's face as she turned to look at Bonner, frowning.

"I know you too well," she told him suddenly. "Despite what you say, something's troubling you."

He would have denied it, but his thoughts were biting deep and all at once they had to be spoken; still, he knew beforehand he was going to be hopelessly clumsy. "All right," he said gruffly. "In the restaurant, earlier tonight, I was watching you talking to one of your customers. . . ."

He could feel her troubled stare studying his face. "I guess you mean Tom Ryan."

"That's right." Already he was sweating a little. "It's not the first time I've seen him there—or the first time I've noticed the way he looks at you. I think you've really got him interested."

Her head lifted sharply. "Will Bonner, are you accusing me of flirting?"

"No, damn it!" he groaned. "But what I *am* trying to say don't come easy." He took a breath, and let the words out in a rush. "The point is, Ryan's a solid citizen of this town. He's got money in the bank, and he's bound to have a lot more before he's done. Maybe you oughtn't to keep discouraging him!"

There was a long moment, while the sounds of the night surrounded them. Jenny lowered her eyes from his face, and she said in a small voice, "It's hard to follow you. I thought at first you were being jealous. Now it sounds like you want—want to get rid of me!"

"Jenny, I want—" He almost blurted, I want you to marry me. But that would have sounded like a proposal, which he was in no position even to consider making; so instead he finished, lamely enough, "I want you to think about the future. Right now you're young, and strong; like you said, a little hard work ain't going to hurt you any. But, what of the years ahead? Remember what you were telling me about the Douglases. You

142

can't go on slaving away, running that restaurant forever."

"I have no intention of doing it forever."

"Unless you're careful," he warned, "it could turn out that way. Time slips by and leaves us standing where we are—and next thing, we're trapped. But a man like Tom Ryan could maybe save you from that, if you'd only give him some encouragement."

Jenny said, in a small voice, "I see. . . ." Suddenly she turned from him, moving as though with impulsive blindness, and started to open the gate. But Bonner's hand was there to trap it and hold it closed against her.

"No, Jenny!" he exclaimed, desperately, to the top of her head as she stood with her back to him. "You *don't* see! What *I* see is that I've no right taking up so much of your time, even if you were willing to let me. Trouble is, I just never thought enough about my own future—or of what I was doing to you. I had my job, and I liked things just the way they were. But it couldn't go on forever.

"I was offered a bribe, tonight," he went on, letting her have it all. "I didn't take it. If I had it might have been big enough to take care of us both, for a long time to come. Only, I couldn't sell out my conscience, or John Isely—and I didn't think you'd have wanted me to, either."

"Of course not," she said, looking down at her hands clutching the top of the gate.

"Still, if John can't be helped to see the mistake he's making, a few more weeks and I'll likely be out of a job. I'll find another one of course," Bonner said

143

quickly. "That doesn't worry me. But it came over me tonight, even a foreman's pay ain't enough that he can think seriously about—you know, about starting a family, things like that.

"I just don't see how I could have been so blind," he went on doggedly, "as to think things could go on like they were. Now I can't even guess what happens next. Cattle is all I know. I'm not sure I can change—and it wouldn't be fair, asking any woman to wait while I found out." He hesitated, finding the courage to add, "Or to pass up any better chances she might have!"

There—it was said, and he felt as though a leaden weight had settled on him. Standing beside her, he watched her in the faint glimmer of the moonlight, seeing only the soft curve of a cheek that told him nothing.

Then she stirred slightly, but without turning to him or lifting her head. "All right, Will," she said. "I know that wasn't easy for you to say. I guess I should thank you." He saw her shoulders lift to an indrawn breath. "And now—will you let me through my gate?"

He dropped his hand and stepped back. There was the slight squeal of a hinge as the gate opened; and then she was gone, hurrying from him toward the dark and silent house.

He knew this had been the end of something; deep regret settled in him as he turned slowly away.

A crow took off from the lower branches of a cotton-wood, virtually exploding from the thin screen of trees and willow scrub lining a dry creek bottom, some half mile ahead of Will Bonner. His eye lifted involuntarily to watch it beat its way across the hot, white sky, its raucous voice quickly fading. Then he looked again at the place where it broke into view, as he sent his dun horse ahead along the trail without altering its easy gait.

Within the past few days these had suddenly become uneasy times for the cattlemen of Cheyenne, thanks to constant rumors of Indians being seen below the North Platte treaty line. There was always a danger of course from parties of hostiles—young bucks, generally, on lightning raids to run off horses or cattle, or perhaps murder a stock tender or two caught off guard at some remote cow camp. But this summer of 1874, with a military expedition under Colonel Custer known to be headed into their sacred Black Hills, it was no surprise at all to Will Bonner that the Indians should be alarmed and resentful, more than ready for trouble with any white men within reach. So he was in the saddle again, having brought out reinforcements to a couple of the more remote camps.

For the better part of two days he had ridden scout with a handful of armed men, hunting fresh sign of unshod ponies, or of any Isely cattle slaughtered or driven off. All appeared quiet, the rumors nothing more than rumors—a false alarm. He had left the reinforcements, nevertheless, and was riding back alone with the steady wind, and the fierce sun scorching the rolling prairies.

Still, if his mind had not been full of the thought of Indians he might have been less alert, now, when he saw something as apparently natural as a crow taking flight from the limb of a cottonwood.

His recent wariness was still with him, however, and it told him something—not necessarily an Indian—must have sent that bird squawking and protesting from its perch. As he considered, his eyes narrowed and his dark face took on a chiseled sternness. Anyone, looking at him just then, might really have decided there was something fiercely Indian about this Will Bonner, himself.

If an enemy should be waiting for him in the willow fringe, he didn't want it guessed that he suspected anything. His belt gun stayed in its holster and his rifle in its place on the saddle. Unhurriedly he rode down a slight slope of grass, browned by summer drought and shining in the sun, and ahead of him the sand strip of the creek bottom drew steadily nearer. A few hundred yards this side of it, the trail dipped abruptly into the head of a shallow wash paralleling the creekbed. Bonner took the drop, but immediately he was below the level of the prairie he pulled in at once and dismounted, grounding the dun's reins and sliding the rifle from its scabbard. Here the crumbling bank rose a little above his head, masked with scrub. Finding an exposed root for a foothold, Bonner removed his hat and cautiously hoisted himself for a look.

Yonder at the creekbed crossing, dry sand glittered in the sun, almost blindingly, and the fringe of cottonwood and willow growth showed indistinctly black against it; but as he studied the scene between lowered lids there was no movement he could make out, except for the stirring of wind across flickering tree heads. Still, he waited, reasoning that if someone was really hiding here they should be wondering, about now, why he had failed to reappear where the trail topped out of this shallow wash. If they got uneasy enough, they might betray themselves.

Suddenly his patience was rewarded. Something moved—a figure, black against the sand sparkle—that crossed an open gap in the willows and was gone almost before he saw it. Bonner had his rifle ready, barrel shielded by the brush so as not to catch sunlight on its blued metal. He made a convulsive move to snatch it up, before he saw his target had already vanished. He let the weapon lie where it was, as he deliberately forced tension out of his nerves.

With the sun beating down and the eroded bank threatening to crumble under him, he continued for minutes longer to study the willows. But the scene in front of him lay as empty now and as silent as before, and when his eyes began to burn and water from staring too long he swore and dropped back into the bottom of the wash. He picked up his hat, as he debated, and drew it on. To the right this wash quickly played out, but it deepened in the other direction. On a decision Bonner took the reins and, not mounting, started that way, leading the dun and carrying his rifle by the action.

It was perfectly quiet here. Loose silt dragged at his boots and muffled the sound of the animal's hoofs, and the heat that set the sweat streaming was almost like something tangible he had to wade through. When he paused to listen he could hear nothing but the sweep of wind through brush above his head, the buzzing of a fly, an occasional trickling as dirt or rocks let go and dribbled down the steep and nearly vertical sides. He could be completely alone, for all the evidence to the contrary—the only human being within miles of this desolate stretch of prairie; he began to grow irritable and impatient, wondering if he *was* alone now and simply wasting his time.

Moreover, he didn't like the direction this draw seemed to be taking. He had assumed it was an early tributary of the dry streambed that he could follow to a place somewhere ahead where the two would join. That way, if someone was still waiting for him at the trail crossing he might be able to come in and take him before the man had a chance to realize he'd been flanked. But now it seemed to Bonner the wash was veering too far to his left, as though to swing wide around the base of a brushy hill whose top he could just see rising against the sky. If that was the case then it probably had no connection with the streambed at all, and his stratagem wasn't going to work.

He was not in a mood now to be satisfied simply at escaping a possible ambush; his anger was up and, besides, he needed to know just what it was he'd nearly stumbled into—in particular, to whom he owed this little diversion. Somehow, he kept picturing Vic Spence and the hatred in the little man's bloody face the night Bonner sent him down the stairs. And yet it needn't be that; it could turn out he had other enemies. For example, it might be one of Frank Keenan's men waiting yonder. To Bonner that made a lot of difference; he couldn't let it go without at least trying to find out.

There was a place where the draw's crumbling bank had been broken down by movement of stock across it, and it looked the likeliest point to climb out; he decided to chance it. The dun had some difficulty with the loose rubble—Bonner had virtually to haul it out behind him, on the reins, the horse bobbing its head and digging in its hoofs. As he came up onto the level, leading the animal, his careful attention was on the creekbank willows and on the mica-glittering stretch of sand beyond.

He doubted that he would be visible, here, from the place where he'd first thought he spotted an ambusher; nevertheless he moved the horse around in front of him and laid his rifle across the saddle while he gave the willows a careful search. He noticed that to his left, at the base of the brushy hill, there was some thick growth that might serve as a screen and give him an approach to the ambusher's blind side—if, in fact, the man was still there. Accordingly, Will Bonner reached for the stirrup, preparing to mount.

At that instant the crack of a rifle broke the stillness. A geyser of dirt erupted as a bullet struck short yards in front of his horse.

The frightened dun tossed its head and tried to shy, adding to Bonner's trouble as he jerked around, as startled as the animal and searching to locate the rifle. Echoes bouncing deceptively off the rise of the hill yonder made that impossible, except that he was nearly certain it hadn't come from the creekbed off to his right.

It meant he was caught in the open, helpless under the sights of a sniper who could zero in on him at any moment.

Then the second shot came, and the dun's frenzied squeal told it had at least been stung. Hampered by his own rifle, Bonner felt the reins slip through his fingers. He yelled at the dun but it had already broken free and was skittering away across sun-browned grass. He let it go; sinking to one knee, he brought the rifle to his shoulder. This time he had glimpsed a film of powder smoke, fast dissolving in the stir of hot wind above the line of brush at the foot of the hill. Had the rifleman been less impatient, a moment later and he would have had his target riding directly into the sights. Now, dark face hard with anger, Bonner fired at the growth, levered and fired again as fast as he could jack out the spent shells, determined the ambusher should have a taste of his own tactics. His shots slapped their own rolling echoes against the rocky hill face.

And then something seared his right arm with the bite of a branding iron. It was the first startling hint that he faced two enemies—worse, that he was caught in a cross fire between them. Shaken by the throb of pain, he hunted the creekbank and saw the shape of a man standing in full view, looking at him down the barrel of a second, smoking rifle. That weapon had the range, and so would the other one directly. Bonner was thinking only of finding cover as he blundered to his feet. He had forgotten the lip of the dry wash, close behind him. The ground gave way beneath his boots; it crumbled under him and suddenly he found himself twisting and spilling in a loose avalanche of cascading dirt and rubble.

He landed flat on his back, for the moment too stunned by bullet shock to think clearly. The sound of a horse's hoofs approaching brought him out of that—belatedly, as he lay there, it came home to him his enemies would be closing in to finish him off. His rifle had been lost in the tumble; he groped for it, without locating it. Then, gritting his teeth against the pain in his arm, he felt for the holster that was half trapped beneath his right leg, found the smooth wooden handle of his revolver, and dragged it free.

A shadow fell across his face. Someone was looking down at him, from the rim of the wash, and Will Bonner lifted the hand gun and fired twice without taking aim, straight upward. He thought he heard a yell, but didn't know if either bullet had found a target; still, the shadow fell away. Coughing on powder smoke that hung chokingly about him, he tried to push to a sitting position but loose silt slid away under his hand and he dropped back weakly.

And now the figure of a second man appeared, black against the sky.

Bonner recognized him instantly—it was Vic Spence. He saw the rifle, its long barrel slanted down at him. It was a target he could hardly miss. Elbow propped against the ground, he thumbed off a hasty shot just as the rifle spoke.

The bullet was a lucky one. It took Spence, half turned him; the weapon flew from his grasp. And the little gunman doubled forward, hit the edge of the bank,

151

and came rolling limply down it. Bonner didn't have to see him light to know he was dead. As a youngster in his teens, he had spent the last year of the war fighting for Texas; he had shot other men, and seen them fall just like that.

There wasn't time to think about him, with an enemy still unaccounted for and only one bullet left in his gun. The realization spurred Bonner and brought him scrambling to his feet, and he caught sight of the saddle gun he'd dropped, its tube a dazzle in the sun. He snatched it up, shaking it free of dirt, and shoved the nearly empty revolver into its holster. And he went charging up the gap in the gully wall, not knowing but what he might run headlong into a bullet.

Instead, it was to see the back of a rider spurring hard toward the willows along the dry creek. Erd Dunbar, he thought. Watching Vic Spence killed must have lost him his interest in this fight, and now he only wanted out of it. Will Bonner set his boots and put a couple of shots after the fleeing man to help speed him; they both missed, but they must have had their effect. The rider ducked his head and drove his horse crashing through the willows, and when a branch raked the hat from his head he let it go, not stopping to retrieve it. His animal's hoofs sent up a glistening spray of sand as it bucked its way across the dry creek.

Then the man was gone, and quiet settled.

Still a little dazed, and wincing as he became aware of the pounding the rifle's butt had given that bullet-creased shoulder, Will Bonner lowered the weapon. He looked dully at Vic Spence's bay horse, standing nearby on ground-anchored reins, and at his own dun that had stopped some distance away and fallen to grazing—it couldn't have been too badly hurt by the bullet that stung it and sent it bolting.

As he stood there in the sun, he thought of Spence lying dead in the bottom of the gully behind him. And suddenly the full impact of what he had just been through hit Will Bonner hard, and left him shaking.

XIII

For all its reputation as a tough town, even Cheyenne was not prepared to watch indifferently as a horse was led down Central Avenue with a man's blanket-wrapped body lashed face-down across its saddle. The sight halted men in their tracks, to shout questions at Will Bonner and, when he didn't answer, to turn and be towed by curiosity for a distance along the plank side-walks before giving it up and staring after him. Their questions meant nothing to Bonner. He was, after his long ride with that grim cargo at the end of his saddle rope, still bitter and appalled over what had happened—and short-tempered from the throb of the hurt arm he had bound as well as he could with his neck-cloth.

He paid scarcely any attention to anyone along the street, until he started to pull wide around a saloon corner and noticed the man coming out through the swinging door, between the beer shields. He had been one of those with the New Mexico herd, and on an impulse Bonner drew over and called to catch his attention. "You—Felton!" The man looked at him above the sleeve with which he was wiping foam from his mustache. Bonner reined up in front of him, and the dun took the opportunity to dip its muzzle into the moss-scummed water of a handy trough.

"You know where to find Showalt?"

Slowly, the man lowered his arm. "I reckon," he answered gruffly. His eyes were pinned on the unmistakable burden lashed to the saddle of the bay.

"Then give him this. Tell him I figure it belongs to him—at least, I'm damned if *I* want it!" And he tossed down the end of the lead rope.

Felton caught it out of the air, as though by reflex, his eyes still foolishly staring. In back of him someone who had started out the door of the saloon suddenly jerked around and plunged back in again raising a shout. Passers-by were beginning to stop to see what was going on. Already a small beginning of a crowd had taken shape.

Now Felton broke free of his tracks. He stepped forward, put out a hand to draw aside the blanket so he could lift the dead man's head for a look. Startled, he let the head flop back again as he exclaimed, "It's Spence!"

"Correct," Bonner answered crisply. "If Showalt, or the law, or anybody else wants to ask questions, they can hunt me up at the doctor's office. I've got an arm needs tending." He lifted the reins, would have ridden on leaving Felton with Spence's horse and the body; but at that instant Trace Showalt came bursting out of the saloon, three more of his trail crew following.

"Bonner!" The angry shout held him. Showalt's head swung, deep-set eyes gleaming as he recognized the body strapped to the other horse. "Is this your doing?"

Will Bonner favored him with a cold look. "If you mean, did I kill him—I certainly did. But happens he forced me into it, him and the other man that tried to help lay a trap for me."

Showalt's tough face was thunderous. His jaw thrust out and he said thickly, "I think you're lying!"

"Do you?" Bonner kept his tone even.

"Even supposing Spence had wanted your hide—and I can believe that, after hearing how you threw him down them steps a few nights back. But, hell! He'd never have asked for help with the likes of you. He wouldn't have needed it."

"That's possible," Bonner agreed. "Unless those were his orders."

"Orders?" the big man thundered. "Now we know you're talking hogwash!"

It was hard not to rise to the baiting, given a temper already shortened by undigested anger and by the pain of his arm. Showalt was being the man-breaker, for the benefit of his audience, but Will Bonner had no intention of giving him what he wanted. He shook his head. "You're pushing it too hard, Showalt," he said calmly. "I won't oblige you." And he neck-reined his horse away.

The trail boss wasn't to be denied. He strode clear out to the edge of the street as he raised his voice in a shout:

155

"Bonner, I'm calling you a liar! Maybe I'm calling you a murderer!"

That could not be ignored. Will Bonner stiffened, and drew hard on the rein. Deliberately, then, he twisted about to give the trail boss his full attention.

Showalt stood poised, his boots set in the mud beside the dripping horse trough, a hand resting on his holstered gun; behind him the men of his crew were plainly waiting to see their boss take another victim apart. Bonner drew a breath into lungs that felt too cramped to hold it. A showdown with this man, at this time, could gain him nothing, and yet he began to doubt that he could avoid it. Showalt had the whiskey sheen in his eyes but he was only drunk enough to be dangerous, careless of any restraint. And if he insisted on making a fight of this—

The decision was suddenly taken out of his hands.

Neither Showalt nor his friends seemed aware of the two newcomers who had appeared at the fringe of the crowd and now came straight through it, making for the trail boss. Bonner saw, and nearly cried out in alarm, Bud, *no!* It was already too late. Bud Dorn, with Pete Gage at his elbow, had reached Showalt, coming up behind him. Bud still had the bandage wrapped around his skull; his words came oddly between unmoving jaws. "You really want to pull that gun," he suggested, "then you just go ahead!"

The trail boss jerked about and saw the revolver pointed squarely at him. He stared at it, and at the man he'd pistol-whipped. His own callused paw was still wrapped around his gun butt: now Bud Dorn said

156

sharply, "All right, suppose you take that thing out of the holster—but do it slow!"

Will Bonner couldn't see the look on Showalt's face, just then. Still, the tense line of his shoulders was expressive enough as, carefully, the trail boss did as he was told—but he was clearly not ready for what came next. When the long barrel of the gun was free of the leather, Bud Dorn nodded approvingly and added, "Now drop it." And he indicated the water trough beside them. "In there . . ."

Showalt's whole body seemed to give a jerk. "No, damn you!"

The gun muzzle pointed at him showed no wavering, nor did Bud Dorn's bruised features within their frame of bandage. The trail boss swore furiously but then, with protest and outrage in every move, forced himself to put out his arm and let his six-shooter plop into the scummy contents of the trough. And now Bonner did have a view of his face, and he read the baffled rage in it.

Bud Dorn, for his part, seemed almost to swell. He might be an even-mannered man, but he was having his revenge and Bonner could see how much he savored it, even while wondering just what the puncher thought he would do next with his enemy disarmed. What he did, in fact, was to step closer to Showalt and, raising his gun, lay its barrel gently alongside the bigger man's jaw. At the cold touch of the metal Showalt's face lost all its color and suddenly shone with a grease of perspiration; he stood ramrod straight, not daring to move, obviously awaiting the blow from that steel tube that would smash bone and teeth for him and repay in kind what had happened to Bud Dorn.

Instead, the cowpuncher gave his cheekbone the lightest of taps with the muzzle, as he said in a mild tone, "Somehow you don't look quite so tough, all at once. . . ." And he stepped back.

At once Showalt lifted both hands, and they were trembling. "By God!" he cried hoarsely. "I'll break you in two!"

"No you won't!" Pete Gage snapped. "You've had your crack at this man; now, back away. All of you!" And Bonner saw why none of Showalt's followers had ventured to interfere up to now—he hadn't noticed the gun the old puncher had been holding on them. The weapon, and his wolfish stare, was an invitation no one seemed ready to accept.

Will Bonner let out the breath that he found trapped in his throat. "All right, Pete," he said. "You too, Bud. You've made your point. Call it off before this goes any farther."

"It's up to them," Gage retorted.

Because of the pistol-whipping of Bud Dorn, there'd been bad feeling and potential trouble from the start between Isely's punchers and the crew of the New Mexico herd. Now these men were watching their boss, evidently waiting for a cue; but Trace Showalt himself seemed unready.

Without anyone quite sure how he knew, it was plain then that the moment had passed, the dangerous corner turned. "Some other time," Showalt promised, his voice still thick with fury. And Pete Gage, seeing there wasn't going to be any challenge, turned his attention to Bonner and to the blood on his bandaged arm.

"You bad hurt?"

"Nothing that can't be fixed up in a few minutes at Morehead's office," Bonner assured him. "But I won't leave the pair of you here. Both of you come along."

"Sure." Pete Gage deliberately put away his gun. "Let's leave 'em this little present you delivered. Me, I want to know what you found out about them Indians."

"So you never ran across no sign at all," Gage said, as he watched the rawboned young doctor finish bandaging Bonner's hurt shoulder. "Well, I figured it for a false alarm but I came in, anyway, when I first got word this morning out at the Butte." He had been ordered a couple of days ago to Owl Butte camp, to oversee construction of new and larger holding corrals.

"It may not always be a false alarm," Will Bonner pointed out, "if we keep breaking our treaties, and hitting the Plains tribes with things like this Black Hills expedition of Custer's. Maybe not this year, or the next—but one of these days, there's apt to be a showdown."

He was seated on a stool in Morehead's operating room, his shirt off and a whiskey bottle in his hand from which he'd been fortifying himself against the pain of having his arm worked on. A few swallows from the bottle had also helped ease some of the tightness out of him, after the confrontation with Showalt.

Though they considered Lane Morehead a good friend, John Isely's men felt some compunction about talking too openly in front of him. But when the doctor stepped out of the room for a moment Pete Gage said bluntly, "Looks to me we got a showdown of our own coming, a lot closer. If Rome Patman ain't declared all-out war, then I don't know what the hell he meant by this try to get you killed today."

"There's no proof that's what it was," Bonner pointed out. "After all, Spence had a personal grievance. Now that he's dead we can't know for certain he wasn't acting on his own."

"But there was two of them came after you," Bud Dorn pointed out.

"True enough. I only got a glimpse of the second one but I had a notion it was Erd Dunbar."

"Another Patman gunhand!" Gage snorted.

"It happens he had a motive, too—or something that could be made to look like one after the other morning, when I laid him out on the depot platform. I've found that a man who depends on his gun usually resents having anybody use their fists on him."

"Then it looks like what we have to do is run the man to earth and get the truth out of him. Was he with Spence today, and was he acting on orders? There's ways even the toughest can be got to open up and talk."

Bonner was dubious. "I wouldn't count on getting anything out of Dunbar. I have an idea, if it *was* him, Patman's going to see to it he lies low for a while—maybe even ship him out of this part of the country, to make certain we don't get our hands on him. . . ."

"So what are we gonna do?" the older man insisted. "Whether we can prove anything or not, we know from

160

now on Patman figures it's no holds barred. You just aim to go on like nothing happened—deliberately make yourself a walking target?"

"Not if I can help it." Bonner corked the whiskey bottle, set it aside. "For one thing," he promised grimly, "after this I'll never again be leaving my gun in my saddlebag!"

Bud Dorn said, "What about the law? With a man dead, surely it's got to take some kind of interest."

Gage started to make some scornful answer to that, but the doctor was back to tell them Bonner had a couple of visitors. He ushered them in: Aaron Pleasants, the city marshal—and Jenny Archer. The girl was breathing hard, flustered and concerned.

It was the first time they had met since their near argument that night in front of her gate; as the doctor discreetly withdrew, Bonner got to his feet and he and Jenny looked at each other, unspeaking, while Pleasants explained, "I was at Jenny's finishing my dinner, when we heard you'd been shot. She wanted to come along."

Bonner thanked her with a silent nod. It was Pete Gage who told the lawman, with dry sarcasm, "Happens we was just talking about you, Marshal."

"Not really," Bonner corrected him quickly. "The shooting didn't happen in town, so that makes it the sheriff's business—not his."

"Better tell me about it, anyway," Pleasants said.

He listened carefully, his cadaverously lean face etched with thought, as Bonner gave an account of the incident, which he edited somewhat for Jenny's sake. "There were two of them," he finished, "and they managed to get me between them. Even so, I'm not all that bad hurt."

"You could be dead!" Jenny burst out. Her face looked almost as white as her shirtwaist.

Aaron Pleasants shrugged bony shoulders. "A lot of things could be, that ain't. Sounds like luck stayed with you, Will. But as you say," he added, "there ain't really anything here I can take hold of, it not being a town business. Nor, to be honest, is there much the sheriff can likely do, either."

"It wasn't in my mind to ask him," Will Bonner said.

Pete Gage had been leaning, with arms folded, against the wall next to Lane Morehead's framed medical diploma, glowering as he chewed at the inside of his lower lip. Now he pushed away to exclaim, irritably, "Damn it, there ought to be some way to pin this on the right party! When Rome Patman brings him in a hired killer, and the fellow tries to do a job on Will Bonner— can it be any clearer he was only doing what he was paid for?"

"It wasn't Patman brought Vic Spence to Cheyenne," Bud Dorn pointed out. "Or the other one either. You'll remember, they both come up from New Mexico with Trace Showalt and the trail herd."

"What of it? Showalt takes his orders from Patman. . . ."

"Not always, he doesn't."

It was Jenny Archer who broke in with that. As they all looked at her she went on to explain, "The two of them were eating in my place one night last week, along with that Morgan Cowley. And they all got into a terrible argument—I don't know what about, but to hear the way those other two were talking back to Rome Patman, and the names they were calling him, I don't see how anyone would have guessed he was their employer. I wondered why he sat there and took it—why he just didn't order them both to shut up!"

Will Bonner was staring at her thoughtfully. "I wonder if you may be onto something! I've noticed, myself," he told the others, "there's something mighty odd about those three—Patman, and Showalt, and Cowley. Catch them off guard, they don't really act like a big operator and his hired men. As Jenny says, they behave more like equals."

"So what's the point?" Pete Gage demanded.

He shook his head. "I'm not sure—except I'm beginning to realize, more than ever, how little any of us actually know about Rome Patman—where he came from, or how he got his money and the herd he brought up from New Mexico. In a new country like this one, those are questions nobody usually asks. You take a man at his face value, especially when he has the cash to back it up. But this time, something's wrong."

Gage said, "What's to be done about it? We're a long way from New Mexico. . . ."

"Well, now." Aaron Pleasants looked around at the others. "I don't know how much this is worth, but it happens I've got friends in Santa Fe. If you want, I could send off a wire—maybe have them put out a few feelers, see what they can turn up if anything. It might be nothing, of course."

"Of course," Bonner agreed. "But for John Isely's sake I'd appreciate this."

"All right, I'll just go see to it." And the marshal put on his derby and left.

When he had gone, Bonner turned to the girl to find her watching him with earnest concern. "Will," she said impulsively, "when I heard you were—" But then she broke off, as though she had just remembered the presence of Pete Gage, and of Bud Dorn, who was seated on the edge of the doctor's examining table, unconcernedly swinging his legs.

Lane Morehead was back, re-entering from his living quarters behind the office. He looked shrewdly at Bonner and Jenny, at the two punchers; he said, "I'm afraid there wasn't much left of that shirt by the time I got through cutting it off you, Bonner. Perhaps your friends could step downstreet to the dry-goods store, and pick you up a new one."

He was looking hard at Pete Gage, who suddenly seemed to get the message and realize Bonner and Jenny might want to be alone. "Oh, sure—sure!" It took a sharp nudge and jerk of the head to bring Bud Dorn off his table. "We'll be right back," Gage told Bonner. "Say, in twenty minutes or so. Come along, Bud."

They were gone, then; and Bonner gave Morehead a nod and said briefly, "Thanks."

The doctor had a final look at the dressing on the wounded shoulder. "That arm will heal fine. Just don't let it stiffen up; keep using it as much as you can. Though if I know you," he added dryly, "that's a piece of advice you don't much need! I've never seen you sit still for very long at a time."

"In my job," Bonner admitted, "a man doesn't. I'll

164

probably be riding again by tomorrow or next day."

"Well, I have things to see to," the doctor said; he left them there, carefully closing the door behind him.

Bonner and Jenny looked at each other in a sudden stiff uneasiness. He knew that she, too, must be thinking of that last scene outside her gate; neither one seemed to know what to say. It was Jenny who broke the silence, picking up what he had told the doctor. "So where will you be off to, tomorrow or the next day?"

"That's up to John Isely," Bonner answered. "He went down to Gray's Fork to look at the New Mexico herd. He said when he got back, he'd want me to ride with him on an inspection tour of his holdings—it's been quite a while since he's spent that much time on the range. This Indian scare may put it off, of course. Otherwise we'll be gone several days."

"Can you? With this?" She meant the wounded shoulder.

He flexed the damaged muscle, gingerly. "It will be all right."

"And are you going to tell him what happened?"

"I haven't decided. I don't know if it would make any difference—if there's anything could change his mind about going through with this partnership. Oh, well," he added, "by the time we get back Homer Nicholls should be home from Omaha, and there'll be nothing more in the way of signing the papers. I guess things will finally come to a head then. . . ."

The words ran out and they were left again in uncomfortable silence. Will Bonner cleared his throat without finding any words, or being able to take his eyes away from her hurt and silent face.

And then, in a faltering tone, Jenny Archer was speaking: "The other night—when you told me to stop chasing after you—"

"I never said that!" he protested, stung. "I never said anything like it!"

"Well, that's what I thought I heard. It did awful things to my pride, Will! I told myself I'd never be so shameless, or so obvious, that you'd have to tell me that ever again—even if it meant that you never came around any more. I guess I just forgot a man doesn't like being chased after, or having a woman make it too easy to see how much she . . . but then . . ." She faltered, and her mouth began to tremble. "But then I heard you'd been hurt, and all at once pride didn't mean anything. I had to come!"

Will Bonner took her into his arms, and felt the warm wetness of tears as she put her face against his chest. He said, with gruff gentleness, "I don't know what I was up to, that night—whether I was being noble, or just plain sorry for myself. The hell of it is, I'm in love with you; I want to marry you, but I don't see now how I'll ever manage it. Nobody knows what's going to happen to any of us—but at least, we can still be honest with each other."

He felt her arms tighten about his waist. "That's all I wanted to hear," Jenny told him, and she sounded content. "Except I want your promise—whatever happens—you'll be sure and take care of yourself! If I can have that, it will do for now."

"It's a promise," he said, and kissed her.

XIV

A faint game trail led down the shoulder of a rocky butte, to a clear-water spring where range animals and riders, white and red, had for many years been coming to drink. John Isely and his foreman followed the trail down, walking their horses carefully, with Isely in the lead and Will Bonner, on Charlie, towing their pack animal.

The spring bubbled out of a natural cairn; the water had a faint iron taste, from minerals in the ground, that was in no way unpleasant. A couple of tall cottonwoods flickered their leaves in the stir of wind that was growing brisker now, suggesting a storm somewhere. The men drank first and then let the horses at the water; Isely stood and pressed his hands against the small of his back, stretching, while he looked about at grass tossing the sun off its blades before the wind's movement. He said, "I think we should rest the horses. Come to think of it, some of that coffee would taste good."

"I'll break out the pot," Bonner said. "See if you can find something to burn."

Afterward, with dry sticks collected and a fire lit, John Isely sat back against a rock and watched his foreman charge the smoke-blackened coffee pot with Arbuckle's and water from the spring. He asked once, "How's that arm today?"

Bonner paused for the briefest moment in his work. "All right."

"Somehow I wouldn't have thought you'd still be having trouble with it."

"Nothing to worry about," Bonner said as he placed the coffee pot in the fire and added more fuel. "I told you, I just sprained it some way."

"Yes, I know. You told me. . . ." But Isely's thoughtful look continued to rest on the younger man.

He seemed in no hurry to ride on, though it would be a good four hours' journey to the next stop in their tour of inspection. Watching him, as they took their time enjoying the coffee, Will Bonner wondered if Isely was beginning to find this riding—three solid days of it, now—more than he could handle. Somehow he had an idea it was more than that. His boss seemed troubled by unspoken thoughts—thoughts he wanted to bring into the open, but so far could not.

He set his cup aside, shook his head at Bonner's offer to refill it. Instead he dug out his pipe and began to pack it. The stillness was complete except for the burbling of the spring, the rustle of branches overhead, the sounds of their horses pulling at tough prairie grass.

Isely said suddenly, "I guess I'm getting old. This has been a pleasant three days—almost like old times; but I can feel it."

Bonner swirled the coffee in his cup. "Well, it looks like we'll have you back in Cheyenne tomorrow, on schedule. I don't think I've shown you anything that wasn't as it should be."

"You've been doing a damned fine job—without too much help from me, I'm afraid, these last months. I appreciate how much I owe you."

"I tried to do what I was hired for."

Isely frowned at his pipe, making no move to light it. "Six years," he said finally. "Well, we were in at the beginning, weren't we? We've seen changes—and there's going to be more. The open range is nearly finished. Time's coming when a man will only be able to run cattle on land he actually owns, and with fences to keep them there. Us early comers, who built to a big scale on free grass—we're gonna have to pull in our horns.

"Only fair, I suppose," he conceded, without rancor. "The new people have their rights, too. I think even an old reprobate of a range pirate like Frank Keenan sees that—but there are some that will go down fighting, before they give up a square inch. There could be real bloodshed."

Will Bonner nodded grimly. He knew the men Isely referred to—men to whom the cattle business, in this new region, hadn't been so much a zestful way of life as a fertile field for greed. When the time came that they were told they must give up all the range they'd held without patent or legal claim, some of those men would resort to guns and delaying acts of violence before yielding to the inevitable. All that still lay in the future, and it might take years for the process to work itself out; but he had already heard the dark rumblings of talk in some of Cheyenne's bars, and he knew with so much wealth at stake the transition wasn't going to be an easy one for Wyoming Territory.

"You're right," he said. "There's changes ahead—no getting around it."

"And those who live through them will need good sense and hard experience, and patience maybe most of all." Isely had dug out a match. He snapped it alight and puffed flame into his pipe; his voice came between drags at the much-chewed stem, as he added, "That's why I'm hoping you'll reconsider what you told me yesterday, and be willing to stay on."

Bonner lifted his head and looked sharply at the older man, through the blue-gray screen of smoke that hung before his bearded face. "Work for Rome Patman?" he interpreted harshly, and shook his head. "Sorry! I meant just what I said. It's something I've given a lot of thought to."

Frowning, Isely removed the pipe from his lips while he blew out the match and dropped the curl of burned wood to the ground. "Well, now," he said slowly, "I've seen you two haven't exactly hit it off, but that don't need to mean anything. It won't take him long to see just how valuable you can be to the partnership." He hesitated. "If it's more pay will make the difference, I wouldn't be surprised if something can be arranged along that line."

For just a moment, Bonner thought of Jenny Archer and the temptation was very real. But he shook his head. "I think you're dead wrong. Patman would never agree. He has his own candidate for my job."

"Trace Showalt, you mean? That brute!" Isely snorted with scorn. "I admit I don't know what Patman sees in the fellow, but I think I've made it clear *I* won't have him, in any capacity!"

And you really think that settles the matter? thought

Bonner, looking at his friend with something near to pity. But what he said was, "All the same, Patman's told me in so many words that he means to be rid of *me*."

"I'm sure you misunderstood," Isely insisted. "You must have! Honestly, Will—I don't like to say this, but just because you so obviously dislike the man, you shouldn't put wrong meaning to every word he says."

Bonner stiffened. His face a mask, he set his cup on the ground beside him—carefully, because his hand was suddenly shaking. He had been determined not to argue with Isely, sensing it would only anger him. But now he was angry himself, and suddenly convinced that the time had come for plain talk, for putting himself on record even if nothing came of it.

"Rome Patman is a crook!" he said flatly, and saw how the other's head jerked up. He went on, each word a weighted counter in a desperate game: "I've accused him, to his face, of using this partnership as a way of robbing you blind—and he never denied it. Instead he offered me a bribe if I would forget my feelings and quit bucking him, and when I refused, he sent a pair of his men to lay for me and try to kill me. If you want to know, that's what really happened to this arm I said I'd sprained!"

He indicated the mending shoulder. Isely's stare was pinned to the younger man's face. His own face looked heavier, bleaker, older; his eyes were almost hidden beneath the downward drag of his brows. He demanded harshly, "And why didn't you tell me the truth?"

"Why? Because it's plain you've already stopped listening to me! You don't want to hear anything that

171

might persuade you against going through with this partnership." He shrugged. "Well, Homer Nicholls will have got back from Omaha by now. I meant to wait and let him tell you how he was threatened and manhandled, and hauled off the train to keep him here by force—but now I wonder if you'll even listen to *him!* All the same, *that's* the kind of men you're dealing with, John. If you just don't want to see it, I ain't sure I know what anybody can do to make you!"

He broke off, struck by the waste of words. The two old friends eyed each other across the dying fire. Isely's face had turned to stone; Bonner didn't know what to expect in return for his blurted speech—a tongue-lashing perhaps. Instead, without a word, the older man suddenly hoisted himself to his feet and, turning his back, walked away from the spring, the rank grass whipping about his legs.

Bonner looked after him, seeing the rigid set of his shoulders, reading outrage in the swing of his arms. Isely came to a halt, staring off over the sweep of Plains toward a black cloud edge that showed darkly, now, across the northern horizon. A strengthened wind came out of the sky, combing the grass and whipping up the tree branches and bringing with it a definite scent of rain. And Will Bonner set himself to work, with mechanical movements, dumping the remains of the coffee onto the fire and cleaning the pot and tin cups at the spring. He brought the horses up, stowed the utensils away, and relashed the pack animal's tarp. He was finishing this chore when John Isely returned and stood a moment silently watching, his bearded features unreadable except for the clenching and untightening of his jaws.

All at once he was speaking, in a gruff voice that hardly sounded like his own. "Could be I'm something of a mule; that should be no news to you, after all this time. But maybe I'm not quite as blind as you think. I can see the chance I'm taking, doing business with somebody I don't know any better than Rome Patman. I see, too, that you're thinking of my own interests— and maybe even risking your neck to do it. I'd be a fool if I wasn't grateful."

Will Bonner knew there was more to come, and that it was costing his friend a real effort to say it. So he waited, and Isely drew a breath and plunged ahead. "Trouble is, answers don't always come straightforward and easy. Maybe I really *am a* fool, Will. At least, one thing I know I am is a man in love with his wife; and there's nothing I can do about *that*. I've told you how she hates this country, hates the cattle business. She isn't going to change—and Will, I can't bear to lose her, whatever else it means I have to give up! A deal with Rome Patman, whether it's a good deal or a bad one, is the only way I can see to give Vinnie what she wants—so you see, I figure I've got no choice." He repeated it, his tone flat with stolid conviction. "I've got no choice at all."

He had raised his eyes, at the last, and was peering squarely at his foreman. The look, more than the words, told Bonner how definitely his mind was set. "Then I guess there's nothing more to argue about," Bonner said.

Isely swung away, stared again toward the cloud swelling on the northward horizon. "A storm's blowing up," he announced. "It'll hit by nightfall."

"We better be going on."

But the older man shook his head. "No." And as Bonner looked at him in surprise: "I think I've seen plenty—I can take your word for the rest. But I can't manage another day in the saddle, not at my age, especially with the weather turning. I want to go in now. If I push it I can reach Cheyenne by dark."

Observing the droop of his shoulders, it occurred to Will Bonner that this was really the end; never again was John Isely apt to mount a saddle, or take another personal look over the scattered reaches of the cattle kingdom they had built together. That time was lost— and so was the fight Will Bonner had been waging, to save Isely from his own misjudgments and from whatever scheme might be working inside Rome Patman's devious brain.

But all Bonner said was, "You're the boss. I'll go in with you—Morehead will be wanting another look at this shoulder." And he turned to tighten Charlie's cinch. John Isely knocked the dottle from his pipe into a bare palm and tossed it to the wind, and stuffed the pipe back into a pocket of his coat.

As Isely predicted, the storm held off during the hours of their silent ride into Cheyenne; but toward the last it seemed to be chasing them in—a sheet of black that swept across the sky, taking the light from the day, and turning the sun's setting into a murky, lurid flare of purplish red that was quickly swallowed up in darkness. Long before that came the flickering of lightning and, in the distance, an occasional muttering thunder that reminded them of cannon fire heard a long decade before, in a war in which they both had served though on opposite sides.

Cheyenne's lights came in view, reflecting off the low cloud canopy; they felt the first stinging drops and caught a rich smell of dust stirred by the fingers of the rain. The shuttling of lightning was eye-punishing now, and the wet wind drove at them hard and the thunder crackled almost overhead. Just as the first buildings of town met them, a Plains storm opened the floodgates above Cheyenne.

They came splashing down the alley in back of Carey Avenue at a fast pace, slickers gleaming wetly, and drew up behind the horse barn at the rear of Isely's property. Bonner dismounted and got the door open and then they were inside, the barn wonderfully dry and quiet after the buffeting of the rain and wind outside. Having lit a lantern and hung it back on its nail, Bonner said, "You go on in. I'll take care of the animals." But Isely had already fallen to, stripping the saddle and gear off his own mount.

Working without talking, they got all three horses into stalls, and forked grain for them. "We'll have Vinnie fix us something to eat," John Isely said. "No sense of your going on downtown until this has stopped. And there's that letter from the Chicago dealer I want you to read."

"All right," Bonner answered shortly. He was in the

bleakest of moods.

Against the streaking spears of rain only a few lights showed in windows of the big house, upstairs or down, to indicate anyone was home. They crossed the yard and gained the side door, shaking rain from their slickers and stomping their boots to dislodge the mud that clung to them. Now that he was home, after three days gone, it was plain to Bonner that John Isely could hardly contain his eagerness to see his young wife. He was calling her name as he led the way into the living room; there the lamps were burning, glowing richly on polished woods and on the elegant gold filigree of Lavinia's harp, but the room was empty. "She must be upstairs," Isely told his foreman. "Make yourself comfortable while I run up for a minute. I'll be right back."

As his footsteps hurried up the stairs, Bonner stood in the middle of the room listening to the peppering of rain against the windows and looking at Lavinia Isely's portrait above the mantelpiece. Suddenly, he had a vague sense that something wasn't quite as he would have expected. He frowned, trying to sort this out. Then he caught, faintly but definitely, the odor of cigar smoke lingering in the room where John Isely's pipe was forbidden. Bonner puzzled over it, somehow not yet really alarmed.

And at that moment he heard, overhead, a man's angry voice shouting and another answering it, a confused exchange that ended abruptly in the report of a gunshot, thunderous within the walls of the house—and, hard after that, a woman's piercing scream. The sounds froze him where he stood; then, without exactly knowing how, he was out of the sitting room and into the entrance hall, and already pounding up the stairway.

There was a landing, with a window paned in diamond shapes of colored glass, and a turn. Taking this, he had a glimpse of the upper hall through the carved spokes of a banister. It was lighted only by the stream of yellow lampglow from beyond an open door, but that was enough to show John Isley's body lying on the hallway carpet. Standing over him, without tie or coat and with the shirt hanging unbuttoned over his deep, black-matted chest, Rome Patman looked toward the stairs as Will Bonner came lunging up them, pawing at his holster. The gun in Patman's grasp was still spilling a trail of smoke as he lifted it now and fired, point-blank, at a distance no more than a few feet.

At the last moment Bonner tried wildly to twist aside, even as he got his hand on the grips of his revolver and pulled it free of the leather. Muzzle flash, directly in his face, blinded him; the trapped roar of the gun was deafening. Dimly he knew that the colored window on the landing below him had gone out, smashed by the bullet. At the same time, his own hurried turn had thrown him off balance. Fighting to stay on his feet, he found himself stumbling helplessly backward down the half-dozen steps to the landing. His injured shoulder struck the frame of the smashed window with a jolt that sent pain through him, and instantly numbed his whole arm to the fingertips.

It should have been easy to finish him off as he stood dazed, unmanned by pain. Perhaps Rome Patman actually thought the bullet had passed through his body before it struck the window, and held off a second shot waiting to see him fall; if so, it was the only thing that saved Bonner's life. He could no longer even feel the weight of the gun hanging from his useless arm. But the cold, damp wind through the opening at his elbow, and his hatred of the man who loomed above him, helped to clear his head. It was with a tremendous effort of will that he reached across with his other hand, took the gun in it and fired, left-handed, into the dazzling smear of afterimage.

Immediately he drove forward, recklessly charging those remaining steps as he contrived, with left-handed awkwardness, to thumb the hammer back and throw a second shot after the first. He expected to meet a bullet, but he gained the upper hall and, strangely, there was no sign of Patman.

He had to clutch at the railing while he coughed on the bitter drift of gunsmoke that surrounded him, and waited for his vision to clear. To his left a lighted doorway drew his attention; through it Bonner saw Lavinia Isely kneeling on a rumpled bed with a sheet clutched about her and her eyes staring at him without focus, blinded with shock. Bonner dismissed her, searching for Patman—and, toward the rear of the black hallway, thought he heard a sound of fleeing footsteps and pushed away from the railing.

He had never been here on this second floor, but he had often noticed a narrow set of back stairs that descended from the upper reaches. Now, as he arrived at the end of the hall, lightning beyond a rain-spattered window showed him the door standing open on a black pit of a stairwell, and he heard someone half scrambling down. Quickly he went in pursuit, his own boots making racket enough to cover any sound of the man he was after.

Below, the side door that he definitely remembered closing stood wide open now, on the stormy blackness of the night. Bonner pushed the screen aside and plunged through, but after that could only halt and place his back against the wet siding, his senses full of the thunder and wind and rain sound, and the constant play of lightning that shone on a thousand vague surfaces and then let them be swallowed up again in darkness.

Rome Patman, too, had vanished completely. It could only be that Bonner's madly stubborn charge up the stairs, coming as it did hard upon the disastrous shooting of Isely, had somehow unnerved the man and driven him to take flight. Still breathing hard, but beginning to think more clearly now with the coldness of the rain that plastered the hair against his skull, Will Bonner holstered his gun. Gingerly he touched his aching shoulder, and turned back into the house.

Anxious as he was to take up the chase, he must first find out how it was with John Isely.

XV

He lay sprawled upon his back, head thrown back and eyes closed and face pale enough for death; but, having brought a wall lamp from its bracket and set it on the floor, Will Bonner could make out a faint lifting of the chest within the shirt that was already soaked with Isely's blood. On her knees beside him, his wife had the bed sheet awkwardly clutched about her in a way that showed Bonner a good deal more of Lavinia Isely than he had ever expected to see. At the moment, he could hardly have been less interested.

With hasty movements he got his friend's limbs straightened, and then ripped open the shirt and sucked in his breath as he saw the damage done by Rome Patman's bullet. It had punched a hole just below the ribs, on the left side, and the blood was flowing freely. A horrified moan broke from Lavinia; Bonner glanced at her, saw that her cheeks were deathly pale between the wings of blond hair that had fallen in disarray. Her mouth worked, her blue eyes were pinned in horror on the bloody wound. She lifted a delicate and trembling hand and pressed it to her face.

Bonner said coldly, "Your husband's alive—no credit to you! If I hurry I just might get the doctor here in time." As he straightened to his feet, there was a sudden racket from the knocker on the big door, belowstairs. "Someone's heard the shooting," he said. "You'd better get your clothes on!"

When the blonde woman gave no sign of heeding, Bonner impatiently caught her by an arm and hauled her up, unceremoniously turned her and shoved her toward the bedroom. After that he hurried down the steps. He got the latch open and flung the door wide.

A couple of figures, rain-soaked, showed dimly in the shadows of the veranda—he recognized a next-door neighbor of Isely's and his gangling son, a half head taller than his father. "What's goin' on here?" the man exclaimed. "We thought we heard shootin'—couldn't be sure, with all the thunder. But I told my wife—"

"You heard, all right," Bonner told him. "Isely's upstairs, bad hurt; I've got to go after the man that shot him. Do you suppose your boy could fetch Doc More-head—fast!"

"Consider it done." The man gave his youngster a push to start him off, with dire warnings against loitering on the way. He added, "What about Mrs. Isely?"

Bonner said, "She's all right, but she's had a bad shock."

"I'll go fetch my wife. Won't take but a minute. Mrs. Isely ain't been what you'd call a sociable neighbor, but a time like this she'll need a woman." And he was gone to get her, with no time wasted in empty questions.

A man of considerable common sense, Bonner decided, who could be entrusted to handle things here. Meanwhile Rome Patman was escaping, losing himself more surely in the stormy night with every moment that passed. Bonner left the door open for the neighbor; he took only long enough to replace the spent loads in his revolver, and to collect his hat and slicker from the nail where he had hung them in the back hall. He stepped out into the rainy dark, with nothing better than guess-work to guide him.

Resaddling Charlie would cost him too much time; he struck out on foot along Carey Avenue, heading for the center of town, and trying as he went to put himself in Patman's place. What would the man do now? Try to brazen things out, maybe—or recognize that his scheming had come to an end and, with a murder charge perhaps facing him, that the only choice left him was to get out of Cheyenne at once, under cover of this storm. Bonner had to assume the latter. Still, there were two places he could think of where Patman might be expected to take the risk of stopping first.

The nearest, if least likely, was only a few blocks away. Bonner covered them at a sprint, along rain-wet and nearly deserted streets with the buildings around him seeming almost to tremble in the steady downpour and smash of thunder and the constant, shuttling flicker of lightning. The hotel blazed with light, but on such a night there was far less than the usual flow of traffic through the lobby doorway, and very few horses and rigs tied up at the hitching rails in front. Cheyenne had sensibly taken cover.

Entering, Bonner glanced at the desk but the clerk was busy. He didn't wait. He was making for the stairs, his boots tracking mud and his slicker shedding rain water onto the expensive carpet, when someone hailed him. He turned as the city marshal, the lantern-jawed Aaron Pleasants, came hurrying from the direction of the hotel barroom. He was plainly excited about something—as excited as his placid nature would allow. "Bonner!" he exclaimed. "When did you get in? I was told you wouldn't be back in town till tomorrow."

"The storm chased us in," Bonner told him. He added bleakly, "Some other people were surprised, too!"

"This came within the hour." The marshal was thrusting at him a fold of yellow paper he'd dug from his shirt pocket—a telegraph form. Will Bonner was impatient but he took it and looked at the message taken down in the scrawl of the local operator, the writing already blurred somewhat by the rain that had soaked into it. By the second word, he had forgotten his impatience:

"Two men you name Patman and Cowley fit description of pair that waylaid and robbed army paymaster of thirty thousand dollars near Las Vegas last winter. Third man masked so cannot confirm description but sounds reasonable it could be one you say is Trace Showalt. Please apprehend all three and hold pending motion for extradition."

As he read the words again, fitting this to what he already knew or had guessed, Bonner was aware of Pleasants speaking somewhere at the edge of his attention: "So we were right—you were right! They're nothing but a set of cheap holdup men. . . . Well, I've got a dozen men searching the town for them. Luckily I ran into some of your riders and they're helping— right now they're upstairs, checking Rome Patman's room. Nobody in the bar has seen anything of him, or his friends."

As he spoke three men came hurrying down the broad

183

steps into the lobby—Pete Gage and Bud Dorn and Jay Tobin, all looking as out of place as Bonner himself. "Nothing," Pete Gage announced loudly. Then the Isely punchers saw their foreman and descended on him. "I see you've heard the news," Gage said, indicating the telegram in Bonner's hand. "Who'd have guessed, not only Patman but all three of them dandies—wanted for plain highway robbery?"

"You can maybe add murder to that," Will Bonner said bluntly. And he let them have the bombshell while they listened in shocked silence—a cluster of big men in soaked headgear and rough clothing and crackling slickers that seemed almost to fill the elegant lobby. "Not a quarter of an hour ago, Patman shot John Isely. There was some trouble between them," Bonner explained briefly; he had no intention of spelling things out in any more detail, or bringing in mention of Lavinia Isely. "I sent word to Lane Morehead but he hadn't arrived when I left and I don't know how much he can hope to do. John's bad hurt—and Patman got away. I'm looking for him now. . . ."

Pete Gage was first to recover, with a rush of blistering angry curses. "The sonofabitch ain't been here; at least, his key's in the slot and we saw no sign of him upstairs. But, hell! With this over his head, he'll be clean gone from Cheyenne by this time."

"Maybe," Bonner agreed curtly. "The others, too, if we don't move fast. By now, word must have reached Cowley and Showalt that the marshal's on their trail and the game is finished."

Aaron Pleasants nodded his bony head. "I thought of

184

that, too. I've sent a couple of men to check on Showalt's usual haunts. But that Morgan Cowley—I don't know. I just haven't been able to find out much about his habits."

"I dunno if this'll be any help," Bud Dorn suggested tentatively. "A girl I know at the Red Ace told me Cowley had moved in with a friend of hers, over south of the tracks. If I can find out where she lives, he just might show up there."

"Worth looking into," the marshal agreed; and Pete Gage said roughly, "Leave it to Bud and me."

"Better move quick!" Will Bonner cautioned, but the two punchers were already on their way. "We can't afford to waste time, either," Bonner told the marshal. "There's one place I'm almost certain Patman would have to stop, though the time element's already against us." He gave a glance to Jay Tobin, who had remained behind. "You'd better come along."

But when he turned toward the street door, his way was blocked by someone who appeared in front of him. A hand struck his chest, shoving him back a step. Frank Keenan's steely eyes peered at him and Keenan's bull voice demanded harshly, "What's this I hear? That partner of Isely's has done him in?"

Will Bonner answered curtly, impatient to move around the man. "He was still alive when I left him— no thanks to Rome Patman."

Keenan shook his ugly head; surprisingly he looked far more angry now than he had the day he and his men were driven out of the Owl Creek soddy. His heavy jaw was suffused with red as he said harshly, "The bastard!

He can't get away with this! Hell—I've locked horns with Johnny Isely often enough to know, they ain't a better man in the Territory. Let me round up some of my boys and we'll—"

There could be no question that this old adversary of Isely's was completely sincere in his outrage. But Bonner cut him off. "No time to raise an army," he said. "If you want to come with us you're more than welcome. . . ."

That made four in the group that left the hotel and set off grimly through the smashing heart of the storm, tramping two abreast along soaked plankings where sheets of rain engulfed the empty streets.

Bonner had an almost certain premonition of failure when they reached the building that housed Patman's office and he could see no light gleaming behind the windows on the second floor. Nevertheless, with gun in hand he led the way up the steps, the boots of all four raising noisy echoes. He was not in the least surprised to find the door at the top standing open, or to see by a flare of lightning that the room beyond, with its sparse furnishings, was deserted. In the following smash of thunder, which seemed to break almost overhead, they entered; someone found a match and scraped a flame to life.

Its flickering showed them the shadow-filled room. It showed something else—the box safe, with heavy door ajar on an empty interior. A coal-oil lamp had been taken from the wall holder and set atop it. Will Bonner touched a palm to the glass.

"Still warm," he announced, as the matchlight died.

"We could have missed him only by minutes."

In the darkness, Frank Keenan demanded, "What was in the box?"

"Their capital, naturally—all the cash Patman and Cowley and Showalt had left, from the army payroll they lifted down in New Mexico. There may not have been an awful lot of it, what with the front Patman has been putting on around Cheyenne, and after buying that herd he brought up with him. Unless of course they stole that, too."

"Begins to sound more than likely!" Aaron Pleasants commented.

"It's plain, now," Bonner went on heavily, "the whole thing was an elaborate confidence scheme. The three had pooled their shares from that payroll holdup, and set Rome Patman up as the front man with a pile of ready cash looking to be invested. I suppose no one of them trusted the others; that's why they rented this office and a safe to keep their money in, probably all three sharing the combination.

"John Isely was to be the sucker. A couple of signatures on a piece of paper would have given them half ownership of his cattle business—after which, I don't doubt they meant to kill him and take the rest. Only, tonight things went wrong. A minute earlier, and we might have caught Patman when he stopped by to clean out what was left in the safe."

Frank Keenan swore fiercely. "So now what do we do?"

"There's the livery stable," the marshal suggested. "He's got to have a horse."

Bonner shook his head. "He'll already have one—even if it meant taking it off a hitch rack somewhere; Rome Patman would never let *that* hold him up! No," he added, feeling the weight of discouragement, "I'm afraid we've lost him. And the others, too—though I'm damned if I give up while there's still any chance of slamming the gate on them."

"Amen to that," grunted Keenan. "But we won't do it standing here!"

Silently, each with his own bleak thoughts, they filed out of the office and made their way down the narrow stairs.

XVI

Pressed close to the clapboard siding, rain beating against his face and one hand clutching a soaked blanket about his shoulders, Rome Patman watched the four come pouring out of the stairway door and start away along the wooden sidewalk; and he had the savage knowledge that they were searching for him. A brilliant flare of lightning showed them, shapeless in bulky slickers, and it picked out the face of the one he hated. At sight of him Patman's fingers tightened on the leveled gun; he had a good target, and the thunder that broke deafeningly almost before the lightning died would have covered the shot.

But the odds were too great and he had only three bullets left. He didn't dare take the risk. He held off, and the darkness swallowed up Will Bonner and the others, and in another moment they were gone.

He told himself he might still have some shred of good fortune working for him, in spite of everything that had gone wrong tonight. He could, after all, very easily have been trapped, either on the stairs or up there in the office—standing beside the rifled safe, with no way out except the dubious one of trying to shoot his way through. He had missed that, by a matter of seconds. Now the man-hunters had vanished and he was still in the clear.

But also without hat or coat, just the way he'd been forced to flee from Lavinia Isely's bedroom—soaked and chilled to the bone, and still seething over his discovery of the empty safe. Whichever of his treacherous partners it was who had been there ahead of him and cleaned it out, of one thing he was determined: Cowley or Showalt—or possibly both!—had made a mistake, taking advantage of the trouble he was in to steal his share of their mutual holdings and sit back while he was hounded out of Cheyenne, with empty pockets and riding a stolen horse!

The heat of his anger against his partners and against the turn fate had dealt him almost served to warm him, and make him forget a little of his physical discomfort.

His borrowed horse was waiting where he had left it, tied behind the office building. It was not much of an animal but he had been in no position to quibble over a choice. More of his luck, though—in a country where every horseman carried a slicker in his saddleroll—to find himself with nothing better than this shoddy blanket which did him almost less than no good at all.

He clutched it about him as he freed the reins and swung into the wet leather, giving the animal a hard jerk on the bit to punish it for his own misery.

These Plains storms were fierce and sudden, but they could end as abruptly as they started. Ghosting through deserted streets that had been turned to quagmires, Patman had a feeling that this one might be easing a trifle. The wind was falling off and a growing interval between lightning flash and thunder indicated the heart of the storm was passing. He had mixed feelings as to that. It could help cover his escape, and wash out his tracks; on the other hand, with most people keeping under roof it made a conspicuous figure of a horseman riding through the rain with neither hat nor slicker.

He kept to dark alleys and side streets as he took the few blocks south through the town. He had a bad moment when he saw the railroad tracks lying open before him, gleaming faintly in scattered lamplight; but he crossed them boldly enough with his gun ready under the folds of the soaked blanket. One shod hoof struck a rail, a single clarion note that must have carried far through the rain and murk. Still he fought the leap of nerves, and the impulse to kick the horse and get away from there. No one seemed to be watching for him, no one noticed at all. So Rome Patman continued at the same deliberate walk—and minutes later, and some blocks farther on, hauled rein beneath dripping tree branches while he sat a moment peering at the outline of a roof, a blacker shape against the early night's darkness.

The house—it was little more than a shack—sat a little apart from its neighbors, and to all appearances might have been deserted. But Rome Patman had been here often, and he knew how effective a blanket hung across a window could be in shutting away any hint of light within. So he dismounted and cautiously approached, and when he was near enough could make out a faint pencil line of light beneath the closed plank door and hear a low rumble of voices. Patman tried the door, and found it latched. Without hesitation he put a fist against the rough panel, hard.

The voices broke off. He pounded a second time, and a woman demanded, "Who is it?"

"Open this damn thing!"

He heard the scrape of the wooden bar being drawn clear. At once he shoved the door wide, and entered.

The shack was crude enough, built of unfinished lumber with muslin tacked across the rafters for a ceiling. A door stood open on a second room, mostly filled by a cheap iron bedstead and a wooden dresser. The main room held a deal table and a few straight-backed chairs, a small iron stove for cooking and heating, a sink, and a packing-case cupboard nailed to the wall. The blankets draped across both windows gave the room a secretive, smothering atmosphere that was heavy just now with the smells of burning pine and kerosene, and brewing coffee.

The woman who had unfastened the door fell back as Patman slammed it open. She might not have been bad-looking at one time but life had been hard on her; in a shapeless pink wrapper, with uncombed and fading hair

191

half covering her sagging features, she watched Patman sullenly but his attention was on the pair of men, seated at the table, who stared at him as he filled the doorway. Trace Showalt was first to find his voice. "You're really a sight!" he grunted.

Patman was suddenly conscious of how he must look—like something dragged in out of the storm. Scowling, he whipped off the sodden blanket from around his shoulders and tossed it aside, pushed back wet black hair that lay plastered to his head, wiped a palm down across his face. He had caught sight now of the object he was looking for—a worn traveling bag, sitting on the far end of the table. He might have expected to see it open, and greenbacks stacked and being counted. Instead, Showalt and Morgan Cowley seemed more interested in the china mugs of coffee they were drinking, apparently lacing it from the half-filled bottle of whiskey on the table between them.

As Rome Patman started toward them, Cowley cursed and got quickly to his feet, saying sharply, "What's got into you?" He moved around Patman to the door and, after throwing a glance into the wet darkness, closed the door and shot the wooden bar into place; turning, he exclaimed, "What's the idea, leaving that open? No telling who might have followed you!"

"Nobody followed me," Patman said shortly. He had backed a step and swung to keep Cowley in sight. Now he jerked his head toward the table and ordered, "Just get back over there—where I can watch you both."

For the first time they seemed aware of the gun that had been revealed when he threw aside the blanket. The two men and the woman stared at it for a wordless moment. Then Cowley's face darkened and he obeyed the order, demanding as he stood again beside his chair, "Just what is this?"

"Maybe that's what *I* intend to find out," Patman retorted. "Sit down. . . . Now, tell me, which of you was it decided to clean out the safe?"

Cowley saw the direction of his glance, then, toward the traveling bag; his expression said that he was beginning to understand. "It was me, as a matter of fact. Hell, somebody had to do it—and fast. After word of the telegram had had time to spread all over town, we wouldn't dare to go near that office. The money would have been lost for good."

Patman's attention had stuck fast at a word that puzzled him. "Did you say 'telegram'?" And at the blond man's nod: "What are you talking about?"

A mutter of retreating thunder was the only sound as the other two shared a look of puzzlement. Trace Showalt was the one who said slowly, "Hell, Morg! He really doesn't know. . . ."

"Then he's the only one in Cheyenne that doesn't!" Cowley indicated the woman, who had put her back against the wall and was watching the scene without any expression in her stolid, raddled features. "Aggie, here, heard about it and managed to tip us off so we could take cover. But we aren't safe, even here—no telling when they might find out about this place and track us down. It seems somebody wired New Mexico and they've tied us to that payroll job. Marshal's got a whole crew out scouting the town for all three of us."

As he absorbed this, Patman dragged out a chair and slowly dropped into it, stunned by the news. He looked at the others; he said slowly, "But I just don't see who could have caught on."

"No? I'd be willing to make a guess," Cowley said blackly; and Showalt, with a scowl narrowing his sunken eyes to pinpoints, nodded as he took it up: "Bonner! That's the sonofabitch—and to think, if Spence hadn't muffed the job we'd been rid of him!"

"Well, Spence and Erd Dunbar just weren't smart enough," Patman said bluntly. "And so here we sit. . . . Pour me a cup of that," he told the woman, indicating the coffee. "And it better be hot—I'm frozen to the bone."

As she sullenly got another cup and filled it from the iron pot on the stove and brought it to him, Patman considered his companions and wondered if they were thinking the same thoughts—remembering another table in a saloon five hundred miles away where they had sat together, three strangers thrown together by accident: Patman, a confidence man fallen on poor times; Morgan Cowley, a gunman on the make; Trace Showalt, finding trail jobs hard to come by as prospective employers learned more about his methods and were increasingly chary about hiring him . . . no one of the three really trusting the other, then or now, but all of them looking for the main chance and willing to pool their individual and peculiar talents, if a likely opportunity arose. . . .

Cowley, at least, seemed to be thinking along such lines; for he shook his head and said, "Starting from nothing, the way we did, we almost made it; call it the luck of the draw. We might as well cut our losses."

"Looks as though we even lose that herd we threw in the pot," Trace Showalt commented bitterly.

Cowley hefted the bag. "And not a hell of a lot of cash left. What do we do with it?"

"I say split it," Showalt said. "And get the hell out of this town, now that the deal is shot to hell."

Rome Patman, with his gun lying in his lap below the edge of the table, had laced his coffee generously from the whiskey bottle and taken a couple of swallows. It worked at the chill inside him, just as the breathless heat of the room helped dry his rain-soaked clothing. Now that he knew his partners had not, after all, been trying to steal the contents of the traveling bag for themselves, he could feel almost friendly toward them. Setting down his cup he said, "If it will make you feel any better, the deal was shot anyway."

They both stared at him. "What do you mean by that?"

Morgan Cowley demanded. His pale eyes narrowed; he seemed to take in, for the first time, the other's disheveled appearance—without hat or tie or suit coat. "Just what the hell have you been up to? You come busting in here like something was after you. What *were* you running from, if it wasn't the telegram?"

Patman shrugged. "If you want to know, I think I just killed Isely. He came home a day early and found me with his wife. I had to put a bullet in him."

"You had to *what?*" Suddenly the gunman's features darkened; he pushed back his chair as his stare bored into the other. "Why, damn you! You're telling us you went and threw it all away—everything the three of us were working for—just because you couldn't keep your hands off that blond iceberg!"

Rome Patman's head swung around. "Watch your tongue!" he snapped coldly. "I knew what I was doing. Even if the partnership deal had gone through, as planned, we couldn't have taken the next step and got rid of Isely, unless we were sure his widow wouldn't be trying to fight us at every move. This was my way of making sure of her, and except for a bad break it should have worked. But after the telegram," he pointed out, "it doesn't matter now anyway, does it?"

Trace Showalt for one wasn't ready to let it go at that. He was glaring at Patman with a look, almost, of pure hatred. "It makes this much difference!" the trail boss retorted harshly. "All along you've gone and set yourself up as the brains of this outfit. You've treated us both like we was little better than idiots, anytime one of us happened to make even the slightest mistake. And then, at the last—"

"You've said enough!" Rome Patman interrupted; his crisp voice and the set of his mouth beneath the black mustache were a warning.

"At the last," Showalt plunged ahead, "you had to go and pull the worst bone-head stunt of all—letting yourself get caught in some dame's bedroom, like—"

The sound of the shot was deafening in that tiny room. For a moment, mouth still open on the unfinished sentence, little eyes staring blankly at Patman, the trail boss sat unmoving. Then, as curls of powder smoke began to drift up above the edge of the table, Showalt's eyes glazed and his jaw slackened and he slumped sideward, limply; he sagged against the table edge and slid off it, in a loose tumble to the floor. And Rome Patman brought up from his lap the gun with which he had gutshot the man, and turned the muzzle, still smoking, on Morgan Cowley.

"I warned him to quit talking," he said without emotion. "Now, put your hands on the table."

Cowley looked at him, and at the gun; he had been caught entirely by surprise and he had no choice. Slowly he lifted both hands and spread them, palms down, in front of him. "So this is how it all ends?"

"It appears that way." Patman indicated the woman, without taking his eyes off the other man. "I suggest you warn her—if she doesn't want to see you dead, she had better behave herself."

"Aggie will do as she's told." A note of strain had entered the gunman's voice; a few beads of perspiration showed at the edge of the yellow hairline above his temples. It was obvious, with the example of Trace Showalt lying gutshot on the floor across the table from him, that Morgan Cowley knew perfectly well death was looking at him from the black muzzle of the smoking gun.

Silence, returning, was heavy and complete except for the snap of a burning stick in the firebox; a gust of wind struck the house, shook the windows and stirred the blankets that covered them, but it carried no spattering of rain to rattle against glass—seemingly, this storm had at last blown over.

Keeping the revolver steadily on target, Rome Patman kicked back his chair now and got to his feet. He reached for the bag, hefted it to judge the weight of its contents, and shook his head. "You were right. There's not a great deal left, is there? Not really enough, after all, to have split three ways. Or even two." And he watched the other's eyes for a reaction.

He got it, a tightening of the gunman's stare. But Cowley said nothing, and Patman explained patiently, "You'd only squander your share, on cards or on some whore like Aggie, and end up no better off than you are. But at the same time there should be enough for a stake in the hands of a smart fellow, operating alone."

The lips barely moved, in the mask of Morgan Cowley's ruddy face. "Go on, you bastard—take it. I'll catch up with you someday."

Just now, though, he sat like a statue, not a tremor of a muscle to indicate he might brave the black muzzle pointed at him. Seeing this, Rome Patman let a smile quirk one corner of his mouth as he started to back toward the door, carrying bag and ready gun. There was a canvas jacket hanging from a nail beside the window; it belonged to Trace Showalt, to whom it would no longer be any use, and Patman halted long enough to set down the bag while he helped himself.

In the moment that he took his eyes from the man at the table, he heard the faintest warning whisper of sound.

His head jerked about and he saw that Morgan Cowley already had the gun from under his coat—he was that quick of movement. Coolly, Rome Patman fired with plenty of time. His bullet took the other man in the chest and brought an anguished shriek from Aggie as she saw him slammed hard against the back of his chair. The unfired weapon struck the edge of the table and came spinning across the room to land almost at Patman's feet. By some miracle the hair-trigger action failed to be jarred off; Rome Patman, reminded that his own gun had no more than one bullet left in it and that he had no reloads, stooped and picked it up.

Morgan Cowley was dead in his chair, head dropped forward onto the table; the woman stood with both hands splayed across her face and her eyes fixed and staring, almost like someone demented. Giving neither one of them further thought, Patman shoved Cowley's gun behind his waistband and took down the jacket from its nail, knowing it would be a size big for him but better than no protection at all against the night ride ahead of him. Encumbered by coat and gun and bag, he got the bar on the door pulled back and slipped outside, leaving the woman and the two victims of his bullets— he had forgotten them almost before the door closed behind him, shutting away the lamplight.

The night smelled fresh after the stink of powder smoke. Patman set his bag down long enough to shrug into the jacket, and then stood a moment testing the darkness. Though the wind that struck him was damp, there was nothing left of the rain except a busy dripping from the roof behind him, and from the trees that tossed against the black sky; lightning still shuttered at intervals but no thunder followed—the storm was passing on.

It was time he did the same.

He started for the place where the stolen mount was tethered. A strong gust struck him, tore at his clothing, and threatened to rip the hair from his head and snatch away the traveling bag with its freight of money. As he halted to brace himself against it, the wind just as quickly dropped off to nothing at all—and in the sudden quiet a voice reached him, startlingly loud: *"He's coming for the horse!"*

Halted dead in his tracks, Rome Patman held his breath as he probed the darkness. The voice had been just ahead—no, it had been somewhere to his left. . . . All at once the night, where a moment ago he had been alone, seemed filled with his enemies. He could hear them in every sound of swaying tree and bush, and the sweat broke out, despite the chill, as he cursed himself for a senseless and uncharacteristic loss of nerve. At the same time he thought of the nearly empty revolver and he dropped it into a pocket of the canvas coat, dragging out the other from behind his belt. Morgan Cowley, he knew, would always carry a ready and fully loaded gun.

He saw he was going to have to give up any idea of attaining the borrowed horse: They would be waiting for him—and besides, if they had any sense at all they must by this time have moved it out of reach. So it was useless to plunge ahead, and pointless to stand where he was. He made a right turn, at random, and struck out in a new direction, moving through blinding blackness and with every sense strained to catch a hint of his enemies' whereabouts.

After three steps he blundered straight into a bush and

for a moment it seemed to grapple him, with thorned and coldly dripping arms. He was almost in a panic before he managed to tear lose and back free, panting a little now with tension and effort. The night was so noisy that he told himself no one could have heard him thrashing; nevertheless he must move on, and fast. He circled the bush, putting it behind him. He thought he had his bearings now. Somewhere just to his right there should be another house, though it must be dark or he would have some glimpse of a lighted window. . . .

Thunder rumbled distantly. And then, as he took another step forward, a shuttering of lightning lit up the night once more with its flat and shadowless brilliance, and he saw the suckered figure that stood motionless under a tree not a dozen feet in front of him. He knew that the lightning showed him as clearly, in his borrowed coat with the bag hanging from his left arm. And as the darkness closed in once more, Will Bonner spoke:

"You'll never get away alive, Patman. You might as well surrender."

"Not to you!" he heard himself shout in a voice that didn't sound like his own. "Not ever!" Another flicker of light, like an echo of the one before it—and Rome Patman fired, twice, at the target it had showed him.

An answering shot smeared his vision with muzzle flame—aiming, he dimly guessed, at the double flash of his own gun. Something struck him a solid blow, and then there was pain that grew until it encompassed the whole stormy night, and then there was nothing at all.

XVII

The maid, dustcloth in hand, met Bonner in the entrance hall and answered his question with, "I think the mister's feeling better this morning. They told me you was to go right up."

"Thanks," he said, and hat in hand he climbed the steps, turning past the landing where a sheet had been tacked over the smashed window. As he turned to the door of the bedroom, he was met by a smell of strong antiseptics mingled with another odor—he recognized John Isely's favorite pipe.

Isely sat propped up against the pillows, in the big, carved wooden bed, surrounded by a scatter of newspapers. "Come in, Will—come in!" he said roughly. "I been wondering if you'd get up to see me today. We got lots to talk about."

"Well," Bonner said, "I'm here."

Homer Nicholls sat on a straight-backed chair next to the bed, a brief case in his lap and his plug hat on the floor beside him. He was scribbling on a pad of foolscap and Isely demanded, "Ain't you through yet?"

"Just finished," the lawyer said, putting his pencil away.

"All right." Isely flapped a hand in dismissal. "You run along then, Homer; we can finish our business this afternoon. Leave that," he added, indicating the foolscap sheets Nicholls had started to put into his brief case. "I want to read it over." The lawyer handed him the pad, snapped his case, and picked up his hat as he rose, moving with customary brusqueness. He gave Bonner a friendly nod, which the latter returned, and a moment later he was gone.

"No need of you sticking around either, Vin," John Isely said. "Me and Will are gonna be making man talk."

She had been sitting in a rocker by the window, occupied with some sort of needlework. She offered no argument, but got at once to her feet and gathered her materials. At the bed she paused to give a touch to the pillows at her husband's back; she told him, "I'll see about your dinner."

"Sounds fine," he grunted. "I could eat a steer."

As Lavinia turned away her blue eyes met Will Bonner's, briefly, but their former cool assurance was totally missing. Her look was uncertain, questioning, and when he acknowledged it with a brief nod she let her glance slide away; a moment later she had slipped past him and out of the room. Isely motioned Bonner to the chair the lawyer had vacated. "Sit—sit," he ordered gruffly. Bonner moved around the bed and let himself onto the chair, placing his hat on his knee.

Isely showed the ordeal he had been put through. His flesh was pallid, almost waxen, etched with new lines and seemingly fallen back more closely to the bones of his face; Lane Morehead had claimed it was only the basic toughness of the man that had kept him alive while the bullet was dug out of him, and afterwards. Nevertheless today—for almost the first time since the shooting—Bonner detected a hint of returning color.

He asked, "How do you feel?"

"Damned impatient, that's how!" the other grumbled irritably. "It's as though that bullet the doc dug out of me had nailed me to this bed! Four days already, and he won't say when he's going to let me up." He shifted a little against the pillows, and winced painfully.

"You know Morehead won't keep you here a minute longer than he has to. In fact"—and Bonner suppressed a smile—"I doubt he could."

"But have you been reading the papers?" Isely picked one up, skimmed it angrily across the bed; it came apart and strewed the bedroom floor. "We can't figure on the market doing anything to save the cattle business. It's up to us! I *got* to be on my feet, damn it—to look for money to borrow and help us over this hump."

Will Bonner knew his expression betrayed his feelings. "I don't doubt for a second you can do it," he began, "once you have your mind made up. But—"

"But I've changed my tune—is that what you mean?" The shrewd eyes were settled on him. "The other day I was telling you I didn't care any more. Well, I reckon you knew that just wasn't so. You sure as hell did your best to prove it to me—that I'd put too much into this business. Whatever way it goes, I have to go with it. . . ." He looked down at the hands, veined and blunt-fingered, that twisted together in his lap. After a moment he added, "Me and Vinnie had a long talk. So far as I'm concerned, at least, nobody ever needs to know what—what really happened that night."

"Nobody will ever hear it from me, John," Will Bonner said quickly.

The older man nodded. "I figured as much, without you saying it." He lifted his head, then, and Bonner saw the heartbreak in the seamed and bearded face. Isely took a deep breath, and there was something almost of pleading in the look he gave his friend. "Will, I still love her! I think she loves me. It was just that—that damned Rome Patman. . . ." He spoke the name in deep bitterness, and shook his head as though to rid himself of memory. When he continued his voice had changed and become flat and matter of fact.

"We've decided we're going on as if nothing ever happened. Only—we ain't moving to no Denver! *That's* settled! We're staying here—and I'm staying with the business I gave six years of my life to building. We'll live in this house that I fixed up the way Vin said she wanted it." His jaw firmed. "But from now on, I smoke my pipe in any room I damn well please!"

And so saying he reached to the table by the bed for the pipe and pouch Bonner saw lying there. As he worked to stuff rough-cut into the bowl he went on, in an abrupt change of subject, "Now, for business—I guess it'd be simplest just to have you read this—if you can make out Homer Nicholls' scribbling." And he picked up the foolscap pad the lawyer had left, and handed it over. Bonner took it, glanced at the hurried writing. Suddenly his head jerked up; he stared at the other man.

"But, this is—"

"A partnership agreement," Isely finished brusquely. "With your approval I'll have Homer go ahead and draw it up for our signatures." A faint smile touched the bearded lips. "I sort of doubt, this time, he'll be wanting to take off for Omaha!"

The younger man was staggered. He put the pad on the bed and he exclaimed, "I don't understand. You're giving me a half interest—for nothing!"

" 'For nothing,' he says," Isely snorted, and looked at the ceiling. "Aside from stopping Patman from finishing me off, that night. . . . I guess I know who's really kept this operation going lately—with no help at all from me! It shames me that I never thought of a partnership before."

"I just tried to do a job," Bonner protested.

"Yeah—and I have to make sure you keep doing it! You've seen what happens to me when I'm on my own. You don't want me tying up with some other scamp like that Patman fellow, do you?" the older man pointed out with bitter humor; then he turned dead serious. "Maybe it's this bullet, but right now I'm kind of feeling my age—I'll admit I felt it some, those few days we just got through spending in the saddle together. No, Will, I'm doing you no favors. It's for my own protection—I want to be sure I have you around to lean on."

Bonner said sternly, "You never had to lean on anybody in you life!" But he added, "All right, John. If you really want me to sign this, you won't have to twist my arm! Besides"—he hesitated—"besides, I know somebody else who's going to be pleased to hear about it."

"Now, I wonder who that would be?" Isely murmured, and added slyly, "It's coming close to dinnertime. Maybe you ought to get down to that restaurant and tell her."

Bonner was already on his feet; but he lingered to ask, "Is there anything I can do for you, first? Anything you need?"

"Nope," his friend told him, as he snapped a match alight above the pipe's bowl. "*Now,* I got everything." When Bonner looked back at him from the doorway, Isely was settled back complacently, already building a cloud of smoke about his graying head.

Center Point Publishing
600 Brooks Road ● PO Box 1
Thorndike ME 04986-0001 USA

(207) 568-3717

US & Canada:
1 800 929-9108